Soaring with Fallon

Also from Kristen Proby

The Big Sky Series:
Charming Hannah
Kissing Jenna
Waiting for Willa

Kristen Proby's Crossover Collection:
Soaring With Fallon: A Big Sky Novel by Kristen Proby
Wicked Force: A Wicked Horse Vegas/Big Sky Novella by Sawyer
Bennett
All Stars Fall: A Seaside Pictures/Big Sky Novella by Rachel Van Dyken
Hold On: A Play On/Big Sky Novella by Samantha Young
Worth Fighting For: A Warrior Fight Club/Big Sky Novella by Laura
Kaye
Crazy Imperfect Love: A Dirty Dicks/Big Sky Novella by K.L. Grayson
Nothing Without You: A Forever Yours/Big Sky Novella by Monica
Murphy

The Fusion Series:
Listen To Me
Close To You
Blush For Me
The Beauty of Us
Savor You

The Boudreaux Series:
Easy Love
Easy Charm
Easy Melody
Easy Kisses
Easy Magic
Easy Fortune
Easy Nights

The With Me In Seattle Series:
Come Away With Me
Under the Mistletoe With Me
Fight With Me

Play With Me
Rock With Me
Safe With Me
Tied With Me
Burn With Me
Breathe With Me
Forever With Me
Stay With Me
Indulge With Me
Love With Me
Dance With Me

The Love Under the Big Sky Series:
Loving Cara
Seducing Lauren
Falling For Jillian
Saving Grace

From 1001 Dark Nights:
Easy With You
Easy For Keeps
No Reservations
Tempting Brooke
Wonder With Me

The Romancing Manhattan Series:
All the Way
All It Takes

Soaring with Fallon
By Kristen Proby

A Big Sky Novel

EVIL EYE

CONCEPTS

Soaring with Fallon: A Big Sky Novel
By Kristen Proby
Copyright 2019
ISBN: 978-1-970077-06-3

Published by Evil Eye Concepts, Incorporated

An Introduction to the Kristen Proby Crossover Collection

Everyone knows there's nothing I love more than a happy ending. It's what I do for a living–I'm in LOVE with love. And what's better than love? More love, of course!

Just imagine, Louis Vuitton and Tiffany, collaborating on the world's most perfect handbag. Jimmy Choo and Louboutin, making shoes just for me. Not loving it enough? What if Hugh Grant in *Notting Hill* was the man to barge into Sandra Bullock's office in *The Proposal*? I think we can all agree that Julia Roberts' character would have had her hands full with Ryan Reynolds.

Now imagine what would happen if one of the characters from my Big Sky Series met up with other characters from some of your favorite authors' series. Well, wonder no more because The Kristen Proby Crossover Collection is here, and I could not be more excited!

Rachel Van Dyken, Laura Kaye, Sawyer Bennett, Monica Murphy, Samantha Young, and K.L. Grayson are all bringing their own beloved characters to play—and find their happy endings—in my world. Can you imagine all the love, laughter and shenanigans in store?

I hope you enjoy the journey between worlds!

Love,
Kristen Proby

The Kristen Proby Crossover Collection features a new novel by Kristen Proby and six by some of her favorite writers:

Kristen Proby – Soaring with Fallon
Sawyer Bennett – Wicked Force
KL Grayson – Crazy Imperfect Love
Laura Kaye – Worth Fighting For
Monica Murphy – Nothing Without You
Rachel Van Dyken – All Stars Fall
Samantha Young – Hold On

Acknowledgments from the Author

I'd like to dedicate this book to KL Grayson, Laura Kaye, Samantha Young, Rachel Van Dyken, Sawyer Bennett and Monica Murphy. Thank you, each of you, for trusting me with your worlds, and for six incredible love stories to add to the Big Sky world. I will always treasure them.

Sign up for the 1001 Dark Nights Newsletter
and be entered to win a Tiffany Lock necklace.

There's a contest every quarter!

Go to www.1001DarkNights.com to subscribe.

As a bonus, all subscribers can download
FIVE FREE exclusive books!

Chapter One

~Fallon~

"*Namaste.*"

"*Namaste,*" my class repeats. Some of them jump up immediately to get on with their days, and some sit quietly for a few more minutes.

Summer yoga is my favorite. I get to teach classes every morning at the Lodge on the lake, for tourists and locals alike. Some days, we're overflowing with newcomers. And some days, like today, it's mostly familiar faces.

The sun rises early in this part of the world during the summer months, so a start time of seven a.m. is perfect to get the blood moving through our veins, outside in the fresh air with the lake shimmering behind us.

"Sorry I came rushing in late, Fallon," Nina Wolfe says with a smile. She's rolling her mat. "I can't believe I overslept."

"No worries," I reply. "It happens to all of us. I'm just glad you made it."

She sighs and walks over to me, her mat slung over her shoulder. Nina is a pretty blond woman with an athletic body and a happy smile. She moved to Cunningham Falls, Montana, just a few months ago to be closer to her brother.

Who happens to be Christian Wolfe, the hottest Hollywood actor in the world.

Of course, he's married to another client of mine, Jenna.

"How long have you lived here, Fallon?" Nina asks.

"Oh goodness, it must be almost two years now." I blink rapidly, realizing that this is the longest I've stayed in one place in more than five years. "Wow, time flies."

"Was it hard for you to feel like you fit in? To make friends? I mean, I have Christian and Jenna, and I have acquaintances, of course, but—"

"I get it," I say, nodding. "Small-town life is different. There's not a lot of people here, and it feels like there are a lot of cliques."

"Yes," she says with a relieved nod of her own. "And most everyone I know is originally from here, so they have that network in place. I just wanted to make sure I wasn't going crazy."

"You're not," I assure her and pat her shoulder. "And it does get easier. You'll recognize faces and make friends."

I frown as I think about my good friend, Penny, who recently moved to Seaside, Oregon. I miss her.

"Why don't we go get some drinks or coffee or something sometime?" she asks. "I've been coming to your class for months. We're friends, right?"

"Sure." I reach into my bag and pull out a card. "My cell is on here. Just text me, and we'll set it up."

"Awesome." Nina grins and takes a step back. "I also might have some professional things to discuss with you. Pick your brain."

"I'm always happy to have my brain plucked." I wink and sling my bag over my shoulder, walking toward my car. "Have a good day, Nina."

"See you!"

I climb into my Jeep and drive toward my house, which is just a couple of miles away. Sometimes I walk to class, but I ran late this morning.

And I admit, I like the feeling of the sun beating down on me, the wind blowing through the Jeep as I drive.

After the long Montana winter, summer is just what the doctor ordered.

I've just stepped through my front door when my phone rings. I grin as I answer.

"Hey there."

"Hi yourself." Claire, my friend from back home yawns in my ear. "Whatcha doing?"

"Just got home from class," I reply as I brew some tea. "It sounds like you just woke up."

"I did." I can hear the smile in her voice.

"Does that mean someone just left?"

"He left a while ago," she says. "And I don't think I'll be seeing him again."

"What's wrong with this one?" I carry my tea out to my back patio and sit at my outdoor dining table. This spot is what sold me on renting this house. The trees and bushes are in bloom, making it feel like a magical garden.

"He moans weird," she says, making me laugh. "Like an old man bending over to put on his socks."

"Not sexy," I agree.

"Too bad, too. He had a nice body. Ah well, there are about a billion more out there."

"With nice bodies? Maybe not a billion."

"You're right. Are you dating a hot cowboy yet?"

I grin and trace the Drips & Sips logo on my mug. "No. It's a small town, Claire. Not a lot to choose from."

"So when are you going to move on to the next place? Or come home?"

I sigh, thinking it over. I don't think I'll ever move back to Chicago. Now that my grandma's gone, I don't have any family there, and Claire is my only tie to the city. I've been roaming around the country, living in my bucket list towns for the past five-plus years.

"I like it here," I reply.

"You've been there longer than the others."

"I know. I just realized this morning that it's been almost two years. I like the community. I'm making friends. Although, Penny just moved away."

Claire scoffs in my ear.

"What was that for?"

"Fallon McCarthy, you don't make *friends*. You make acquaintances. And even then, getting to know you isn't easy."

"I know," I murmur. That's the way it's always been, my whole life. I'm an introvert. I enjoy my own company more than I like being with others. "People exhaust me."

"Maybe that's why you're better in a small town," she says. "Fewer people."

"That's definitely a plus," I agree. "What are you doing today?"

"I'm going in to work for a bit."

"On a Saturday?"

"Hey, you worked today."

"For an hour. I don't have any other classes today."

"Well, I have some accounts to work on. What are you going to do with the rest of your day?"

"I think I'll go on a short hike," I reply. "It's a beautiful day today."

"Like, on the treadmill?" she asks. "A simulated hike?"

"No, city girl, a *real* hike. In the woods. On a path."

"Do you, like, have hiking boots?"

I smile and tip back in my chair, enjoying my friend. "I have hiking shoes. They're not boots."

"Huh. Well, whatever floats your boat, my friend. Have a good day."

"You, too."

I hang up, go inside to rinse my mug, and put on the hiking shoes that will need to be replaced soon, and drive across town to my favorite hiking trail.

One of the things I like best about Cunningham Falls is all of the outdoor activities here. There are miles and miles of hiking trails that the city keeps groomed and safe for hikers. Last week when I came to walk on this particular trail, it was closed due to mountain lion activity.

That gave me pause.

But I carry bear spray, and the only animal I've ever seen on the trail is a deer.

Halfway up to the lookout point, I get a text.

Nina: *Breakfast tomorrow? 9:00 at Ed's?*

I grin and type a quick reply.

Me: *Sure, see you then.*

Claire's right, I don't make friends easily. I wouldn't even consider Claire my *best* friend. She's a close friend. But the sad thing is, she and Penny are probably the best friends I have, and even they don't know everything about me.

I don't even have a bunch of baggage in my past that would cause my lack of trust in others. No one has betrayed me. Or bullied me.

It's just my nature to hold back. To be the observer and soak everything in.

And because of that, I am sensitive to moods and emotions, and that's exhausting.

So, instead, I've made a habit of being a loner. It suits me fine.

But having breakfast with a new friend sounds fun, too. Maybe I'm just evolving as a person. I'm only thirty-two. A person can change.

I come around a corner and shift to the side of the trail so a runner can zoom past me. He nods in thanks and keeps going.

Nice ass, I think to myself and grin.

I set off again, about to head over the ridge to the overlook. It's a great place to sit and breathe, to watch the lake and the boats floating on it, not to mention the gorgeous Whitetail Mountain above it.

But a rustling in the bushes catches my attention. I reach for my bear spray, just in case, but then pause and squint, trying to see what's going on.

"It's a bird," I mutter, stepping closer. A white head pops up, and I gasp. "A bald eagle. Hi there, sweetie. Are you hurt?"

One wing flaps, but the other doesn't move at all.

The poor thing's hurt.

"Crap, I don't know what to do about this. I'm not ready for this."

I look up and down the trail, but there's no one close by. The runner is long gone.

So, I pull out my phone from my pocket and call Penny. She grew up here, she'll know what to do.

Unfortunately, she doesn't pick up, so in my panic, I call Claire.

"Did you get eaten by a tiger?" she asks.

"There are no tigers in North America, Claire. But I did find an injured eagle. I don't know what to do?"

"Why did you call me?" she asks.

"Because *I don't know what to do.* Tell me what to do."

"Call animal control?"

I frown, watching as the poor thing struggles. "What are they going to do? Fine it?"

"I live in Chicago, Fallon. I don't know. Call 911. Call the sheriff. Call *anyone* but me."

"Thanks a lot." I hang up and take a deep breath. "Who do I call for you?"

A veterinarian!

I Google vet offices in Cunningham Falls and call the first one on the list.

"I'm on the Bear Mountain trail, just outside of town, and I found an injured eagle. What do I do?"

"Oh, you'll want to call Spread Your Wings," the receptionist says. "They'll come help you."

"Thanks." I hang up, not at all sure of what Spread Your Wings is, but a phone number comes up when I Google it, so I call.

"This is Noah."

"Uh, hi, my name is Fallon. I just found an injured eagle." I repeat my location.

"Don't move," he says briskly. "I'm coming right now. How far up the trail are you?"

"I'm maybe twenty yards from the top."

"Of course, you are," he says. "Looks like I'm going for a hike. I'll be there in less than thirty minutes. Can you stay there?"

"I'll wait," I confirm, and he hangs up. "Well, looks like help's coming. Don't worry, they'll get you all fixed up."

I'm talking to an eagle.

I sit on a stump and don't take my eyes off the bird. He's watching me, as well.

"I'm friendly," I say. "And I won't hurt you. How long have you been here?"

He squawks, making me smile.

"Maybe you don't speak English. I'll be quiet. But I'm here with you."

I take two long, deep breaths, trying to calm my heart. If I'm upset, the bird will be upset. I don't know how I know that, I just do.

It's like when you're trying to calm an upset baby.

Not that I've ever had a baby.

"Now I'm being ridiculous," I mutter.

It feels like three hours later when I hear someone hurrying up the trail.

"Fallon?"

"Over here," I call and stand, waving my hands. "We're over here."

A man appears, carrying a huge animal carrier. He's hardly winded, and I know he had to practically run up the mountain to get here so quickly.

"I'm Noah," he says. "Where is it?"

I point to the bushes, where the eagle has finally calmed down.

"He's there. One of his wings isn't moving."

Noah approaches the bird, and before I know it, he's secured something over its eyes and manages to put it in the carrier.

"Wow, you've done that a time or two."

"Or fifty," he says with a smile. "I'll get him down to the sanctuary and have a look. Thanks for calling it in."

"Of course," I reply and watch as he walks away, hurrying down the trail. "Bye."

I look around, not sure what to do next. So, I finish my hike to the overlook and watch the boats, take in the sounds of the woods around me, and then start back down to the Jeep.

What a weird day.

* * * *

"You totally saved an eagle's life," Nina says before taking a bite of her pancake.

"No, I called Noah, and he saved it."

"He wouldn't have done that if you hadn't called. Noah's a nice guy."

"Do you know him?" I ask, trying to sound casual. "I'd never met him before the trail."

"Sure. Noah's good friends with Max Hull and the rest of the Hull family, I guess. I've met him a few times." She stops chewing and grins at me. "He's hot, isn't he?"

"Is he?" I sip my tea. "I didn't notice."

"Uh-huh. Sure. And I'm a coal miner's daughter." She leans in. "He's single."

"How nice for him."

She smirks. "And you're interested."

"How did we get on this subject?"

"You should go see him," she continues. "And check in on your eagle."

I blink at her, thinking about it. "Why would I do that?"

"Because you're an attractive, single woman, and Noah's single, and you should go flirt with him. What will it hurt?"

I frown. "I never said I wanted to flirt with him."

"Fallon, we may not know each other well, but I know the look of a woman who's interested in a man. And when you said Noah's name, you got that look."

"Okay, so he's attractive," I reply. *Yeah, try smoking-hot in all fifty states.* "That doesn't mean I need to go flirt with him."

"Are you dating someone else?"

"No."

A slow smile spreads over her lips, and I feel myself start to give in.

"Fine. I'll go check on the eagle. But only because I'm concerned."

"Sure. That works. Okay, now that I've solved your love life issues—"

"I don't have love life issues."

"—let's talk about something else just as fun. I'm starting a business in town, and I'd like to talk to you about some opportunities."

"I have a full-time gig between the Lodge and the studio downtown."

"Well, just hear me out, and then you can give it some thought."

I nod, and Nina continues, telling me all about the business she's starting with two of her friends from California. A company to help busy women.

"Basically, there may be times that I would call to book an in-home yoga session. We could work around your schedule, of course."

"Interesting," I reply with a nod. "It's something to think about, for sure."

"That's what I was hoping you'd say. Saffron and Lindsey will be here in a couple of weeks, and we're hoping to have things up and running next month."

"Thank you for thinking of me," I reply.

"You're the best in town," Nina says with a wink. "And we want the best. So, think it over, and we can get together anytime to fine-tune things."

"Thank you."

Once I leave Nina, I make my way over to Drips & Sips for my favorite tea. I have my own lemon oil with me to flavor it, ignoring the looks I get from the tourists waiting for their lattes, and then I climb in my Jeep and drive out to the Spread Your Wings bird sanctuary.

I looked up directions this morning before my breakfast with Nina.

Something just told me I should go and say hello.

And I usually listen to that *something*.

The sanctuary is out of town, in the middle of nowhere. Which makes sense because the animals are wild and they need plenty of space.

There's a farmhouse across the pasture from the industrial buildings. And the sign over the driveway says *Spread Your Wings*.

This is the place.

I park and walk into an office area that's currently deserted.

"I wonder if I should have called ahead," I mutter out loud.

"Nah, there's always someone bustling about." I startle at the voice and turn to find Noah standing behind me with a grin. "Fallon, right?"

"Yeah." I reach out to shake his hand and feel the warmth climb all the way up to my shoulder. His hand is callused and large, engulfing my small one. "And you're Noah."

"Guilty," he says. "Did you come to check on your eagle?"

And to check you out.

"I did," I say. "I know it probably seems weird, but—"

"Not weird at all. Follow me."

We walk outside and down a long, paved sidewalk that meanders between several buildings.

"I wasn't expecting it to be this big," I say.

"That's what *she* said," he replies with a grin, and I can't help but laugh out loud. "Sorry, couldn't resist. We've grown a lot in the past few years, thanks to donations and grants. Most of these buildings back here, along with all the concrete sidewalks, are new."

He leads me into a big building and down a row of cages, then stops and gestures.

"Well, hi there," I croon. "How is he?"

"He has a broken wing," Noah says and sighs. "We can't tell what caused it. But I think that with about six weeks of healing time, he should be good to be released back into the wild."

"Really? That's amazing. What if he can't live in the wild again?"

"He'll stay here, with us, and we'll use him for education. He'll have a cushy life here, but I suspect he'll be leaving us. He's a healthy guy."

We're quiet as I watch the bird. He looks at me as if he recognizes me. There's a splint on his wing.

"I'm so glad I found you," I murmur.

"Me, too," Noah says and smiles when I look over at him. "The bird, not me."

"How long have you been doing this?"

"Most of my life, but I started the sanctuary eight years ago. I have a masters in zoology from Colorado State."

"Wow. And you came back to Cunningham Falls?"

He grins, and I feel it in my gut. Goodness, Noah King has a great smile.

"I have roots here," he says. "It's home."

I nod and look back at the eagle. "He's gorgeous."

"You can visit him anytime you like."

I start to decline but reconsider. "You know, I just might do that."

"Good." He clears his throat. "I hate to do this in front of our feathered friend because I'll be embarrassed if this goes badly, but can I interest you in dinner?"

I blink, taken off guard. "Tonight?"

"Anytime you like," he replies with that easy smile. "Tonight. Tomorrow. Right now."

"It's not even noon."

"It's five o'clock somewhere."

I laugh and look down at my feet, then shrug. "Sure. A girl has to eat, right?"

"Exactly. May I see your phone?"

I unlock it and hand it over, and he punches in some numbers.

"I just texted myself. If you text me with your address, I'll pick you up at seven."

"It's a deal."

I say goodbye to the eagle, and Noah escorts me back to my Jeep.

"I'll see you tonight, Fallon."

"See you."

I drive away, the memory of Noah's voice tickling my mind. The way he says my name is like a promise. Like he enjoys the sound of it on his tongue.

Fallon.

It's not like me to accept a date invitation, but there's something about Noah King that I like very much. What will one dinner hurt?

Chapter Two

~Noah~

Fallon intrigues me. I've seen her around town once or twice, and each time, I've stopped to get a good look at her. And when I saw her standing on that mountain, watching over the eagle, I knew I'd ask her out the next time I saw her.

She's a pretty little thing, and I do mean *little*. She can't be much more than five-foot-two, and her body is lean. Petite. Her dark hair is long, and today, she was wearing it down.

It's the kind of hair a man wants to get his hands in, to hold on to.

And when she smiles, and her green eyes light up, well, it hits me right in the gut. I've been thinking about her all damn day.

I'm ready to spend some alone time with Fallon.

I park my truck in front of her little house and walk up the walkway to her porch, then ring the bell and shift back and forth on my feet, surprisingly nervous.

I don't go out on many first dates.

Hell, I don't go out on many dates at all.

I'm focused on work and my family, and I haven't had a lot of time to pursue a woman for anything other than a mutually enjoyable bounce on the bed.

Fallon opens the door, and I feel my jaw drop.

"Wow."

She grins, her green eyes happy as she steps back to let me in. "Wow yourself," she says, not shy at all about looking me up and down, and by the expression on her face, she likes what she sees.

Which is completely mutual.

Her dress is short with orange and purple swirls on the material. It looks soft.

"I'm trying to decide on shoes," she informs me as she closes the door and leads me into the living room. The house is small but furnished nicely. There's no clutter to speak of, and I don't think that's because I came over.

Something tells me that Fallon doesn't keep clutter around.

"What are the choices?" I ask.

"These." She lifts a pair of sexy-as-fuck heels in one hand. "Or these."

The other pair is black flip-flops.

"I know they're not as fancy, but they're comfortable. So my question is, where are we going?"

"I was thinking dinner at Ciao," I reply, imagining her legs propped on my shoulders with those heels on her feet.

Stop it.

It's the first date.

She walks over and stands next to me, craning her neck to look up at me.

"You're what, six-three?"

"Six-four," I reply with a grin.

"I'd better wear the heels." She slips them onto her feet and then looks up again. "Oh, yeah, that's better."

"They do incredible things to your legs," I reply as she walks across the room to gather her purse. Her muscles are toned, and her legs are long, especially for someone so short.

"Thanks." She glances around. "Okay, I think I'm ready."

I escort her to my truck, which I've never had issues getting in and out of, but Fallon stares at it dubiously.

"This isn't a short-girl truck."

"No." I laugh. "Short-girl trucks aren't good for actual work. Here."

I boost her up into the seat, shut her door, and then round the truck to climb in next to her.

"I'll remember to use the SUV next time."

She looks over at me with a raised eyebrow, her lips tipped up at the corners. "Already planning on a *next time?*"

"Hell yes, I am," I reply as I pull away from the curb and drive us into town. I made reservations, so when we arrive, we're escorted right to our table.

"I'm Rebecca," the waitress says, writing her name on the white paper that covers the table. "I'll be your server. Can I start you out with drinks?"

I glance at Fallon, completely at a loss for what she might like. I don't even know if she drinks alcohol.

"I'd love a glass of the pinot gris," Fallon says and smiles.

"I'm happy with a Pepsi," I reply and smile at my date as the waitress walks away. "So, how long have you lived in Cunningham Falls?"

"About two years," she says, reading her menu. "How about you?"

"Since the day I was born," I reply with a smile. "So, if you have questions about anything, or if you need to know who's who, I'm your best bet for information."

"I'll remember that," she says and sets her menu aside. Rebecca returns with our drinks and takes our order, then leaves us alone. The restaurant is busy and loud, but we're at a corner table, away from the hustle and bustle. "What do you like best about living here?"

"Good question." I sip my drink, thinking it over. "Well, my family is here, and it's a big unit. So I like being here in case any of them needs me. I ski, so being so close to the resort is awesome. Do you ski?"

"No. How many brothers and sisters do you have?"

"Just one brother. Gray. He does construction and teaches ski lessons in the winter. But I have plenty of cousins. Our roots are deep here. What about your family?"

Fallon sips her wine, and I watch the way her lips pucker. I'd love to get that mouth on mine.

"I don't really have any family to speak of," she says calmly. But before I can ask for more information, she says, "Did you like living in Colorado?"

"It was fine," I reply. "But it wasn't home."

She just nods.

"How long have you taught yoga?"

"Only for about five years," she says with a smile. "I used to be an accountant."

She frowns as if she didn't mean to give me so much information, and I have to admit, her short answers are frustrating. For the first time in my life, I've met a woman who doesn't want to talk about herself, yet

I want to know all there is to know about her.

"That's very different from yoga."

"Yes, I suppose it is," she says. "Do your parents live around here?"

I frown. "Why do I get the impression that you don't want to talk about yourself?"

Holding her wine glass, her hand pauses a few inches from her mouth. "I'm telling you about myself."

"No," I say, shaking my head. "You're giving me short answers, then turning it back to me. The point of a first date is to get to know each other so we can decide if we want to keep seeing each other." I lean over and tuck a piece of hair behind her ear. "Why so mysterious?"

"I'm not mysterious," she says, frown lines forming between her eyes as she glances down.

"Are you wanted by the FBI? Are you part of the witness protection program?"

She smiles. "No."

"Serial killer?"

"I mean, I do enjoy cereal. Wheat Chex, usually."

"You're a smartass," I say thoughtfully. "I like it."

She laughs. "Pistachio ice cream."

"Go on."

"Pistachio is my favorite ice cream."

"Okay." I lean in, intrigued. For some reason, I get the feeling that Fallon doesn't always share a lot of details about herself. "What is it about that flavor you love?"

"Well, I like the green color," she says with a smile. "And I like that it's not too sweet. Also, pistachios are healthy so I can say I'm eating health food."

"See? This isn't so hard."

She blows out a breath. "Harder than it looks."

"I'm not scary," I inform her, all the humor gone from my voice. "I'm just a nice guy, trying to get to know you better. And now I know that you like pistachio ice cream and green and pinot gris."

She smiles, and I swear it lights up the whole damn room. "What kind of ice cream do you like?"

"I'm a chocolate kind of guy, but I'll take just about anything over at Scoops. Except the huckleberry."

"Wait, you were born and raised in Montana, and you don't like huckleberry ice cream?"

"I know, I'm surprised they haven't asked me for my Montana card. I think I just had too much of it growing up."

"No huckleberry for you then," she says and leans back as our meals are delivered. Hers is a meatless pasta dish with a white cream sauce, and mine is good ol' spaghetti and meatballs.

"Are you a vegetarian?" I ask casually.

"No." She shakes her head, takes a bite, and sighs in happiness.

And…cue my dick. If she makes noises like that when her food tastes good, I can only imagine what'll come out of her mouth when I'm inside her.

"I do try to stay away from red meat and pork," she says with a shrug. "Mostly because they're just not good for heart health. I mainly stick to fish and chicken. Why do you ask?"

"Because, although I may not love huckleberry ice cream, I *am* from Montana, and I love beef. And let's face it, breakfast isn't the same without bacon."

"They do make turkey bacon," she reminds me, and I feel my face crumple into a scowl.

"That just seems un-American."

"Or healthier," she says with a laugh. "Is this going to be a deal-breaker for us?"

"It's not good," I concede and let out a long, dramatic sigh. "But I guess I can overlook it."

"I'm so relieved." Her voice is bone-dry, and it makes me laugh.

"You and I are going to get along just fine."

＊ ＊ ＊ ＊

"I enjoyed myself," Fallon says as I escort her to her door. "And I can't believe we spent three hours at dinner."

"Time flies when you're having fun."

Or when you're talking to a beautiful woman and enjoying yourself more than you have in years.

Fallon stops at her door, and I can see by the look on her gorgeous face that she's trying to decide if she should invite me in or say goodnight.

So, I make the decision for her.

"I'd like to see you again," I begin and take her hand in mine, linking our fingers.

"I'd like that, too," she says.

I step closer with the intent of kissing the breath out of her against the door, but when I move my feet, a sloshing noise catches my attention.

"Shit."

"It's okay," she says, backing away. "You don't have to kiss me—"

"What? No. There's water coming out from under the door."

She steps back, looks down, and reaches for the knob.

"Don't open it," I say. "If it's seeping out, there's a lot of water behind this door. Is there a back way in?"

"This way." She hurries, despite her heels, around the house to the back. The sliding glass door is unlocked and opens easily. We both stop short when we reach the living room.

"Shit," I repeat, staring up at the hole in the ceiling. "Where's the water shut off?"

"I have no idea," she says in shock. "I rent this place from Jenna Hull."

"I'll find it." I hurry outside and, sure enough, find the valve on the side of the house. I turn it off.

"That was it!" she yells from inside, and I join her as we both stare in shock at the damage done in just three hours.

"Okay," I say, taking a deep breath. I watch in surprise as Fallon does the same, matching her breath to mine. "Check your valuables."

"I don't have any," she says. "At least, nothing that can't be replaced."

"I hope you have renter's insurance," I reply. "Most of this furniture is a loss."

"It's not mine. This place came furnished. But, man, this sucks."

"Big time," I agree. "Do you have family you can stay with?"

"No." She doesn't elaborate.

"Well, I have a guest suite. You're welcome to it."

"You don't think I can stay here?"

I stare at her, then look back at the gaping hole in the ceiling, the one still dripping water. The floor is soaked with at least three inches of standing water. "No. It's not safe."

She sighs. "You're right. I can get a hotel."

"I swear, you can use the guest suite," I repeat firmly. "I'm not using it, and it's relatively private. You'll even have your own bathroom."

"Why would you do that?"

"Because that's what we do here. We help each other."

She shakes her head. "You wouldn't last a week where I come from."

"And where's that?"

"Chicago." I watch her thoughtfully as she sloshes over to gather her computer. "At least this didn't get wet."

"Does that mean you'll come to my place?"

"For tonight," she confirms with a nod. "Thanks for the offer. I'll gather some things and follow you out there."

"Let me help."

"It's just some clothes and toiletries," she says. "It won't take long. I'll call Jenna from the car. You can go ahead and go. I'll be right behind you."

"You're sure you're okay?"

She smiles and nods bravely. "This is a piece of cake."

"Then you've been eating the wrong cake," I reply. "I'm going to swing by the store, and then I'll be home."

"Is yours the house by the sanctuary?" she asks.

"That's the one."

"I'll meet you there," she says.

I leave the way we came, through the back door, and rush to my truck. I swing into the grocery store to buy some staples, including pistachio ice cream. When I'm home, and the groceries are put away, I quickly survey the guest suite. The sheets are fresh and clean. I set out towels in the bathroom and make sure everything is sparkling.

It won't do if Fallon shows up to anything less than comfortable.

While I'm waiting for her to arrive, I make a call to my assistant at the sanctuary, letting her know that I may be late in the morning and asking her to find someone to cover the feeding, and then I call my brother, Gray.

"You're not usually up this late," he says.

"It's not even ten yet," I reply.

"I'm just saying, you're not a night owl. What's up?"

"Fallon's going to be staying with me for a few days."

Gray's silent for a moment, and I think the call dropped. "Hello?"

"Is this my brother, *Noah*, who doesn't invite women to his house?"

"You're funny," I reply and quickly tell him about my date with Fallon and finding the ceiling caved in at her place. "So she's going to stay here tonight or until it gets figured out."

"Look at you, mister knight in shining armor."

"It's the right thing to do," I insist.

"Sure." He clears his throat. "So, the date must have gone well if you're asking her to sleep over."

"Why did I call you?" I ask aloud.

"I don't know, why did you?"

I sigh. "Because I like her. I don't know her well yet, but I really like her."

"Then be a gentleman," he says soberly.

"I'm not going to insist she share my bed."

Even though I'd like to. Something tells me we'd be hot in bed together.

But he's right. That's not the way to start something with a woman, and I intend to start something.

"I'm also giving you the heads-up because Jenna will most likely call you to patch the ceiling."

"Sounds good," he says. "Let me know if you need anything."

"Will do. Thanks, Gray."

Chapter Three

~Fallon~

"The *ceiling* caved in?" Jenna asks in my ear. I'm driving to Noah's place, most of my clothes, toiletries, and electronics in the backseat.

I always travel lightly.

"It did," I confirm. "I'm sorry, Jenna. I have no idea what happened, but I'm assuming it was a leak."

"No, *I'm* sorry. Where are you going tonight?"

I bite my lip. "To Noah's."

Jenna's quiet for a second. "Noah King?"

"Yes. We were on a date when we discovered the mess, and he offered me his guest suite."

"Reeeeeally," she says, her voice full of smiles. "Tell me more. How many dates have you been on?"

"Only one," I say with a laugh. "But he seems nice. At least, I hope he doesn't plan to murder death kill me in my sleep."

"He's the best," she says with confidence. "He's one of my brother's best friends. You can trust him not to hurt you. But, honestly, I feel horrible, and I'd be happy to pay for a hotel if that would make you feel more comfortable."

I take a deep breath as I turn down Noah's drive.

"Thanks, Jenna. Why don't you have someone assess the situation at the house, and then we'll go from there? I'm safe for tonight."

"We can totally do that. Have a good night. I'll be in touch tomorrow when I have information. In the meantime, you said the water is turned off?"

"Yeah. I don't think there's anything else that can be done this late."

The sun sets late during the summer, but it's already dark.

"I'll go over first thing in the morning. Thanks, Fallon."

"No problem."

I hang up and put the Jeep in park, staring at Noah's farmhouse. The lights are on inside. He even turned the porch light on for me. Aside from the house lights, the area is pitch-black. There aren't street lights this far out of town. Across the pasture at the sanctuary, there are some lights over the sidewalks.

It's damn dark out here.

Claire would tell me that I'm asking for the murder scene I told Jenna about. That to accept this invitation from a stranger is dangerous.

If I still lived in Chicago, I would agree with her.

But I don't. I'm in Montana. Not that it's crime-free, but Noah knows my friends, and I know that Jenna wouldn't have his back if he were a bad guy.

At least, I hope.

Just as I hop out of the Jeep to gather my things, the front door opens, and Noah joins me.

"Let me grab that," he offers, taking the biggest bag. "This should tide you over."

"This is all my stuff," I say before I can keep the words in my head.

"*All* of it?"

I nod and follow him into the house, taking a long, deep breath once I'm over the threshold.

His home is full of positive energy. It's calm. Happy.

"Did you grow up in this house?" I ask, surprising him.

"Yeah. I bought the place from my parents a few years ago. I've been fixing up a few things, but it's pretty much the same."

I smile. "You have a nice family."

He frowns. "Have you met them?"

"No." I shake my head, feeling stupid for saying anything in the first place. "Your home just feels peaceful."

He cocks his head to the side, and a smile spreads over his handsome face. "Thanks. You're back here. Follow me."

He leads me down a hallway, to the back of the house, and into a large bedroom with a four-poster, queen-sized bed.

"The drawers in the dresser are empty," he continues as he sets my bags on the bed. "And all of the linens are fresh. The bathroom is through here."

He turns on the light, and I follow him, getting a look at a simple tub and shower combo, a single sink and toilet. It's small, but it's been recently updated with pretty, dark fixtures, extending the farmhouse feel all the way back here.

"I'm on the other side of the house if you need anything," he says, leaning against the vanity in the bathroom.

I nod, looking around. "This is great. Thank you. I spoke to Jenna, and she said she'll let me know what we're in for tomorrow after she has someone come out to look at the mess."

"No hurry," he says with a shrug. His arms are crossed over his chest, showing off his biceps.

I have a thing for men's arms. Some women like butts or abs.

I'm an arm girl.

And Noah has *amazing* arms.

"Hello?"

I blink and look up at his face. He's grinning. He knows exactly what I was just thinking.

And I don't care that he knows. I'm attracted to him, and for once in my life, I'm not going to shy away from someone I like.

"You can touch them," he offers, and it's my turn to be surprised.

"I will," I say before clearing my throat. "Eventually."

He pushes away from the vanity and walks to me, slowly, like a lion stalking its prey. Something tells me he's just as powerful as the king of the jungle.

He stops just a few inches in front of me and drags the pad of his thumb down my cheek and over my lips. My breath catches in my throat.

Jesus, Mary, and Joseph he's potent. Sexy and strong. He smells like cedar and whatever kind of soap he uses.

And he's so fucking *tall*. I'm still in my heels, and he dwarfs me.

"Why am I so drawn to you?" he asks quietly, leaning closer.

"Good question," I whisper. Noah's lips twitch before he leans in to cover my mouth with his, softly at first. Barely touching me. But then he buries his fingers in my hair and sinks into the kiss, sighing in delight as he presses my back against the doorjamb. I grip his sides, fisting his shirt in my hands, and moan.

The next thing I know, he boosts me up, and I wrap my legs around his waist, his jeans-clad dick pressed to my core. I *want him.*

I want Noah King with everything in me.

Right now.

But rather than carry me to the bed, he sets me on my feet, steadies me, and then steps away. He's breathing hard. His chocolate-brown eyes are hot and pinned to me as he props his hands on his hips and shakes his head as if coming out of a fog.

A sexy, lust-filled fog.

"If you need anything—" He clears his throat. "If you need anything, just let me know."

I can't reply. I don't think I can form words yet. So, I just nod and watch as he walks to the door of the bedroom.

With his hand on the knob, he turns and smiles at me. "You'd better lock this door, sweetheart."

He winks, and then he's gone, closing the door behind him.

I touch my fingertips to my still-tingling lips. On unsteady feet, I walk to the door and flip the lock.

I don't know if I'm keeping Noah out, or myself in.

Because I want to follow him, strip both of us bare, and beg him to take me.

But I'm not a beggar, and I know he wants me, too. I could *feel* it, in more ways than one.

I lick my lips, still tasting him, and grin as I turn and begin unpacking my bags.

* * * *

The sun is just starting to peek through the windows as I lazily stretch my arms over my head. It's six in the morning, as it is every morning when I wake up. I don't even need an alarm clock.

My eyes pop open every morning at the same time.

I don't know if Noah's up yet, but I don't need to worry about waking him if he's not since I'm on the other side of the house. So, I get up and immediately sit on the floor and enjoy fifteen minutes of meditation and stretches before I get dressed for the day.

After putting my things away late last night, I took a shower and washed my face. I thought of Noah and that melt-your-panties-off kiss for a long while before finally falling asleep sometime after midnight.

Despite getting less sleep than I'm used to, I'm surprisingly bright-eyed this morning as I pad out of the bedroom and down the hall.

Noah's up, and if the smells coming from the kitchen are to be believed, he's been cooking breakfast.

I come up short when I turn the corner and see Noah stirring something on the stove, dressed in only sweatpants that hang loosely from his hips.

In fact, rather than announce my arrival, I lean my shoulder on the wall and just watch his back and arms flex as he moves. His skin is tanned, as I'm sure he spends a lot of time outside, especially in the summer.

And, much to my delight, he has two dimples just above his ass.

I swallow hard and feel my core tighten at the sight of him.

"Do you mind getting some plates out of that cupboard?" he asks, making me jump a bit. He gestures with his spatula. "I can see you in the glass, Fallon."

"I didn't want to startle you," I lie as I breeze across the kitchen and fetch the plates, setting them on the counter next to him. "Where is the silverware?"

"Over there," he says but stops me before I can walk past him. "And good morning."

He kisses my forehead.

Christ Jesus, is this guy for real?

"Good morning."

"Did you sleep well?"

"Like the dead," I reply with a grin. "And you cooked me breakfast."

"It's just some scrambled eggs and toast," he says, then turns his attention back to the stove. "I wasn't sure what you usually eat. There's coffee in the pot."

"I'm actually a tea drinker," I reply as I set the forks on the small table in the breakfast nook next to the kitchen.

"Pistachio ice cream, green, pinot gris, and tea."

"Are you making a list?"

"Damn right." He plates the eggs, turns off the burner, then butters the toast and joins me at the table. "I have earl grey in the pantry, but I don't know how old it is. I think it's left over from my mom."

"It's okay," I reply with a smile and take a bite of the toast. "I'll grab some from Sips later."

"If you tell me what kind you like, I'll pick some up this afternoon."

I stop chewing and stare at him in surprise. "You're so nice."

"I keep coffee for me, might as well have tea around for you."

"I might be able to move home later today."

He just snorts and shakes his head. "It's going to take a few days, easy. So you might as well get comfortable. Unless you don't like it here."

I frown and shake my head. "No, the room is perfect. Thanks for loaning it to me. I'll hear from Jenna later this morning, and then I'll let you know."

He nods once. "What are your plans for the day?"

"I have class pretty much all day." I check the time but don't hurry. "My first class is at eight, and I'll be done around three."

"That's a long day of yoga," he says.

"I'm used to it now." I shrug and pull my legs up under me, watching as Noah's eyebrows climb in interest. "Some of the classes are harder than others. I do beginners' yoga, which is pretty basic and not taxing on me at all. But I also do core yoga, and that can kick my ass."

His gaze roams all over me, and I know he's trying to picture what I must look like under my yoga pants and fitted tank.

I'm proud of my body. I wasn't always in such good shape, although I am genetically blessed with a petite figure. I've worked damn hard to be this toned and strong.

And I have a feeling he'll see it sooner rather than later.

I smile and take the last bite of eggs before I take my plate to the sink, rinse it, and put it in the dishwasher.

"What about you? How does your day look?" I ask.

"I'm usually over at the sanctuary before the sun comes up," he says with a shrug. "And I come home whenever the work is done. Some days, it's by suppertime, and other times, it's after dark."

"I guess that's what you get when you own the place."

He nods and stands, setting his own plate in the sink as he lays a key on the countertop.

"That's for you," he says casually. "It works in both the knob and the deadbolt."

"You're giving me a key?"

"You're staying here, and I don't know when I'll be home later, so yeah. It's just a key, Fallon." He kisses my forehead again, and I'm pretty sure I melt into a pile of mushy goo. "I'd better get ready to head out."

He walks down the hall to his bedroom, and I stare at the key on the counter. Of course, he gave me a key. It's not because I'm moving in with him permanently, but because I'm staying here.

It makes sense.

And it makes butterflies take flight in my belly.

Which is dumb.

"Ridiculous," I mutter as I rinse and place Noah's plate in the dishwasher with mine, then walk into my room to gather my water bottle, mat, and handbag.

When I get to the living room, Noah's just about to walk out the front door.

He holds it open for me, and I step outside, and then I'm suddenly jerked back inside.

"Whoa," he says, pointing.

"Holy shit," I whisper and swallow hard. "That's a bear."

"Good eye," he says, and I elbow him in the side for his smartassery, earning a laugh. The bear's head comes up at the sound, and I freeze again.

"He's going to eat us."

"It's just a little black bear," Noah says softly. "He's just moseying around, looking for some berries."

"Or human flesh," I add.

"He's not a grizzly."

I tip my head back to stare up at Noah in terror. "Do you get grizzlies out here?"

"Maybe once a year," he says. "Too many people."

"Oh, God." I swallow hard. "I don't do well with bears."

"Look, he's walking away."

The beast is lumbering through the yard toward the woods about fifty yards from the house.

"Maybe he lives in those trees," I say.

"Probably so," Noah replies as if it's no big deal at all.

"Maybe I shouldn't stay here after all."

He urges me onto the porch and frowns down at me. "Because of a harmless little black bear?"

"Maybe he's not harmless."

"Did he look ferocious? Fallon, he's a little guy. He was just wandering through. Nothing to worry about."

"If you say so."

"Trust me. I've lived out here my whole life, and no one has ever been eaten by a bear on this property."

I raise a brow. "Is that supposed to make me feel better?"

"Yeah. Did it?"

"No." He laughs and waves as he sets off across the pasture to the sanctuary. "See you later."

I wave back and climb into the Jeep. I have time to swing by Drips & Sips for some tea on my way to the Lodge for my first class, and I can drive by the house to see if anyone's there yet.

Probably not. It's just after seven, for Pete's sake.

But I'm pleasantly surprised to see a work truck and Jenna's SUV parked in front of the house when I drive past, so I stop and knock on the open front door.

"Hey, guys."

"Hey," Jenna says, turning around. "Fallon, this is Grayson King, Noah's brother."

"Oh, hi." I smile and hold out my hand to Gray. "I've heard about you."

"Same goes," he says with a wink. Before I can ask him what he means by that, he continues. "This is pretty bad. Looks like the shower upstairs has been leaking in the wall for some time, and finally soaked through the drywall down here."

"I see most of the standing water is gone." I look around. "I hope it doesn't cause mold."

"It'll be tested before you move back in," Jenna replies. "Gray just said it'll be about three days of repairs."

"Wow." I swallow hard.

"And then I'll have to have the space tested for mold, and we need to make sure everything is dried out, not to mention, I have to replace the furniture. So," Jenna continues, "I'd say you'll probably be out of here for about a week."

"A *week*?" I squeak.

"Sorry," she says and cringes. "I'll totally pay for a hotel if you like."

"I have a place to stay," I reply, ignoring the look that Jenna and Gray exchange. "I'll let Noah know. I'm really sorry about this. I never had any indication that it was happening. I didn't see any drips or a wet spot in the ceiling."

"Not your fault," Gray says. "This is an older house, and my guess is the plumbing hasn't been updated in about twenty years."

"Or more," Jenna agrees. "I should have done that when I bought it."

"But I was too eager to move in," I remind her. "Just keep me posted on when I can move back in."

"Will do. See you at the ten o'clock class," Jenna says with a smile, and I wave as I leave.

Looks like I'll be staying with Noah for a while.

I've just walked into the studio when I check my phone and see a text come in from Penny.

Finally, she's replying to me. She's been gone for less than a week, but I miss her.

Penny: *So I may be working for someone famous, not the plan, remember the band Adrenaline?*

I frown down at the phone. Remember them? They're only my favorite ever.

Me: *TELL ME EVERYTHING, and I thought you were working at a coffee shop. In fact you sent me a picture of you at that very coffee shop yesterday morning? Did you quit? Why aren't you keeping me updated? Also if you don't respond asap you're dead.*

I smirk as I send the message. Claire and Penny are two people who don't mind my bluntness. I haven't seen Claire in years, but Penny is someone I can hang out with and not be exhausted after.

Penny: *I may be working for Trevor Wood as a part-time nanny before his kids start school and I may have said yes without thinking and now I'm staring at my phone like I'm more than the hired help and I'm one day in."*

Me: *Trevor Wood. The Trevor Wood? Hottest drummer alive? Six-pack for days? That Trevor Wood?*

Holy shit! Lucky Penny. But then I think back to Noah and *his* hard abs and I'm not so jealous anymore.

Penny: *Yes, focus! We texted a bit last night, and he was flirty, I was flirty...*

Me: *Aw, did he pass you a note in biology too? Maybe you guys can play MASH later!*

I toss my head back and laugh as I add a house, car, and vacation emoji.

Penny: *Very funny. I need you to virtually slap me so I stop overthinking this. I'm the nanny. That's it.*

Me: *Consider yourself slapped, you're the nanny but that doesn't mean you can't still be open to something more...adventurous. I mean that is why you abandoned us, isn't it? You needed a change of scenery and God in his mysterious ways gave you Trevor Wood! Bitch.*

    Penny*: So…just roll with it?*

    Me*: I want notes at the end of every day. Or I'm killing you.*

    Penny*: I miss you.*

    Me*: I miss you too. Facetime later?*

    Penny*: Yes please.*

    Me*: Preferably when you're at work, I wouldn't be mad.*

    Penny*: Signed an NDA so not a word!*

    Me*: Lips are sealed. Love you.*

    Penny*: You too.*

I slip my phone into my bag and get ready for my first class.

Chapter Four

~Fallon~

It's just not my day.

To start, after my first class, I finally ran over to Drips & Sips to snag a cup of tea, and then spilled said tea all over my hand, burning it.

Then, I had a client wrench her back because she tried too hard, and another class that had zero people show up.

None. Nada.

Of course, that wasn't my last class of the day, where I could have just gone home for the rest of the afternoon. No, that would have been too easy. It was my noon class, so I decided to take myself out to lunch.

Sounds perfect, right?

Wrong.

I found a hair in my sandwich. Yep, one of *those* hairs. Short and coarse, and all I could think was that some guy in the kitchen had just scratched his crotch before he made my sandwich. I just couldn't stomach eating. Of course, I wasn't charged for the meal, but still.

Gross.

My last class started at two. It was usually my favorite of the day because it's a beginner class, and I generally get a lot of tourists.

And I did have a full room, with not one familiar face.

But I also had a group of about five teenagers who were in town with their parents and decided they wanted to try yoga. They laughed, giggled, and mocked me the entire hour, ruining the experience for everyone else.

I asked them not to come back.

So now I'm irritable, my hand hurts, I'm hungry but still grossed out by the pubic hair, and I'm as far away from my center as I can get.

I don't like it.

I hope Noah isn't home when I get there. I don't want him to see me like this. He barely knows me; he shouldn't have to see grumpy Fallon so soon.

I pull into the driveway and let out a gusty breath.

Of course, he's home. Because the Universe is out to get me today.

Noah's just hopping off his lawnmower, covered in sweat and rubbing his sweaty forehead with his forearm as he walks to me.

"Hey, you," he says in greeting.

"Hey, yourself." I try to smile but feel like it falls flat.

"What's wrong?"

I sigh. I can't lie to this guy. And it seems I can't hide my emotions from him either. He calls me out on being evasive, and rather than get annoyed like I usually do, I find myself *wanting* to confide in him.

All of this is a brand-new experience for me.

"Shitty day," I say when he cocks a brow at me. "I wasn't expecting you to be home already."

"I have more volunteers than I know what to do with this time of year," he says, glancing over at the sanctuary. "Summer brings them out in droves, which is helpful, but honestly, all of the people being underfoot makes me stabby. So, I leave them to my staff when I start to get twitchy."

"Best not to stick around." I smile and step up onto the porch.

"Want some company?" he asks as he opens the door for me. "I'll go get a quick shower in first, though. I'm sticky."

"Sure."

He winks and disappears down the hallway.

Did I just agree to company when I'm irritable? It seems I did.

Because, apparently, I'm trying all kinds of new things lately.

I walk down to my room and quickly change my clothes into denim shorts and a fresh tank. The only good thing about not having any boobs to speak of is I don't need a bra, especially when it's hotter than balls outside.

It's crazy to me how cold it gets in the winter, and then just a few months later, it seems Satan himself is vacationing in Montana, bringing the heat with him.

I pad barefoot out to the living room. I'm hungry, but nothing sounds good, so I just sit on the couch and sigh.

It's quiet here. There's no traffic noise, no people walking past the house. It's just silent.

And it's pure bliss.

"I smell better," Noah announces as he saunters into the room. He's changed into cargo shorts and a Spread Your Wings T-shirt. His dark hair is wet from the shower. "So, what happened today?"

"What didn't happen today?" I laugh and pull my legs up under me. "I burned my hand."

"Let me see." He sits next to me and reaches for my hand, careful not to touch the tender skin. "Ouch."

"Yeah. I'll put some lavender oil on it, and it'll heal in a couple days, but it sucked. A client injured herself in class because she was showing off for her friend."

I roll my eyes. Noah rests his elbow on the back of the brown leather couch and listens intently.

"Then, I didn't have *any*one show up for my noon class, so I decided to go out for lunch."

"Nice."

"And found a pubic hair in my sandwich."

"Gah." He makes a choking noise and presses his fist to his mouth. "Jesus, that's gross."

"Pretty gross," I agree and then tell him about the idiot teens in my last class. "It was just a very trying day."

"I have something for you," he says and jumps up, walks to the kitchen, and returns with a small tub of ice cream and a spoon. "Pistachio."

"You bought me ice cream." I stare at it, touched that he thought to get my favorite.

"Just in time for a shitty day," he confirms as I spoon a bite into my mouth.

"I feel a tiny bit guilty for eating this when I haven't had dinner yet."

"You know, one of my favorite things about being an adult is that I can eat ice cream for dinner and no one gets to tell me I can't."

"Get your own," I say, narrowing my eyes at him. He pads back into the kitchen and returns with another small pint of his own.

"There. Dinner's solved," he says with a satisfied grin and takes a bite of rocky road.

He looks good sitting over there, one leg up on the couch so he can face me. He's tanned all over, and there go those arms again, flexing and looking sexy.

"What are you thinking?" he asks and licks his spoon.

Rather than answer, I set my ice cream on the coffee table, take his and do the same, and then I straddle him right here on the couch as if I've done it a million times before.

There's something about Noah that makes me feel comfortable, and I'm not going to overthink it right now.

"I like your arms," I reply as his hands firmly cup my ass.

"I caught you looking at them earlier."

"I know."

"You didn't care."

"Nope. You have good arms, what's to be sorry about?" I lean over and kiss his cheek. The hands on my ass tighten.

"So the chemistry here is off the fucking charts," he says as one hand roams from my butt, under my tank, and then up my back. "And you're not wearing a bra."

"Nope." I grin before covering his lips with my own. The kiss is hot but slow. I'm exploring him, his lips and his tongue, and reveling in him exploring my body. I brace myself with my hands on his strong shoulders, enjoying the way the muscles move under my palms.

The next thing I know, I'm flat on my back on the couch, and he's over me. He's pinned my hands over my head with one hand and uses the other to cup one breast under my shirt, still kissing the hell out of me.

I'm cradling him with my thighs, and I can feel him harden and lengthen. Everything about Noah King is just delicious.

And I want every inch of him.

He finally releases my hands to tug my shirt over my head and tosses it on the floor. His lips instantly latch onto a nipple, making me arch my back, pressing closer to him. Not for the first time, I wish my breasts were more impressive.

"God, you're so fucking sweet," he growls, gliding his hand up and down my torso. "Your skin is soft."

I bury my fingers in his damp hair, holding on tightly as that magical hand unfastens my shorts and slides down to the promised land.

"Jesus, Fal, you're so wet."

"I'm *so* turned on." I moan, circling my hips and encouraging him to push those fingers inside me.

I'm not disappointed.

"Yes," I breathe, clenching onto his fingers and riding him like a woman possessed.

"My God, just look at you," he says, his brown eyes shining with lust. "You're amazing."

"You're doing this," I remind him, just as his phone rings. "Ignore it."

But his hand is already gone, and the orgasm I was reaching for has retreated.

"Damn it," he grumbles. "I'm so sorry. It's my emergency line. I have to answer."

His eyes are on mine as he accepts the call. "King. Yeah. Yeah."

And I see it. He's needed somewhere, and this will have to wait for another time. "Yeah, I'll be there as soon as I can."

He ends the call and immediately covers me again to kiss me silly. But when he pulls away, I see the regret in his eyes.

"I have to go," he says. "I'm so damn sorry."

"It's okay. Where are we going?"

He grins. "We?"

"Hell, yes. You don't get to do that to me and then run off without me. Where are we going?"

"West of town about ten miles, toward the Lazy K Ranch."

I'm not sure what a Lazy K Ranch is. "Can I have my shirt back?"

"Regrettably, yes." He kisses me once more before standing and taking the ice cream to the kitchen. "But I'm taking it off again later."

"Promises, promises."

* * * *

"Babies," I whisper as I climb out of Noah's truck and follow him to the side of the road where an older couple is waiting, watching a cluster of little balls of fluff.

"Thanks for calling," Noah says to the man, shaking his hand. "Fallon, this is my uncle Jeff and aunt Nancy King."

"Pleasure to meet you," I say and smile. I'm quickly shocked to find myself wrapped in a tight hug by Nancy. She pats my back and pulls away with a smile of her own.

They're a friendly family, that's for sure.

"How did you find these guys?" Noah asks as he takes a big pet carrier out of the back of his truck.

"Until about five minutes ago, they were in the middle of the highway," Jeff says, helping Noah herd them into the carrier.

"I shooed them to the shoulder," Nancy says. "What are they?"

"Owlets," Noah replies with a smile. "And if they're out here alone, their mama is probably not doing well."

"We haven't seen a mama," Nancy says, and I immediately feel my eyes fill.

Poor babies.

"I'll get these guys loaded on the truck and take a quick look around," Noah says as Jeff continues helping him load the owlets into the back of the truck. Then we all set off on foot, up and down the highway, looking for the mama.

"What kind of owl would it be?" I ask.

"I think they're grey owls," Noah says. "But when they're that little, there are a couple of possibilities. I think we'll know her when we see her."

I nod and hike off the highway a bit, keeping my eyes open, grateful that I wore my hiking shoes rather than my flip-flops.

"Noah!" Jeff calls, catching all our attention. "Over here!"

Noah reaches Jeff's side first, his face grim.

"Damn," Noah says with a sigh. "She didn't make it."

"I can't look," I say, shaking my head as Nancy slips her hand into mine and we wait back by the road. "I'm sorry, I just can't bear it."

"I understand," Nancy says. "The hardest part about living on the ranch all these years is seeing the animals hurt."

I look over at her and smile softly. Nancy is a lovely woman in her sixties with laugh lines by her eyes and only a touch of grey in her hair.

"Do you still live on the ranch? Is it the Lazy K Ranch?"

"Oh, yes," she says. "We're retired now, and our sons Josh and Zack run the ranch, but Jeffrey won't ever leave it. Noah's parents, Susan and Doug, moved down to Arizona a few years ago for the winters, but I don't think I could talk Jeff into that. And to be honest, I'm okay with that. The winters don't bother me much."

"You're a close family," I say, watching Noah and Jeff talk to each other where the owl is.

"Very," she says with a smile and looks over at me, a frown forming between her brows. "What about you, Fallon?"

"I don't have family," I reply easily and grin reassuringly. "It's not a sad story, and I'm fine. It's just interesting to me when I meet a large, close-knit family."

"Well, you're welcome at the Lazy K anytime."

Noah and Jeff make their way over to us.

"Are you going to bury her?" I ask.

"No," Noah says with a frown. "She'll be taken care of by other critters, just the way it should be in the wild."

"Circle of life," I mutter, thinking it over. I've never thought about it being so sad before.

"Do you know what killed her?" Nancy asks.

"I think she was probably hit by a truck," Noah says with a sigh. "Poor thing. But we have the babies, and we'll take care of them."

"I know you will," Nancy says proudly. "Our Noah is a talented zoologist."

"She has to say that because she loves me," Noah says and winks.

"And because it's true," Nancy says as we walk toward our vehicles.

"I spoke with Doug the other day," Jeff says. "He said he and your mom should be here by next weekend. They're usually home by now."

"I know, but Mom joined a book club, and she wanted to be there for their meeting tonight," Noah says with a laugh. "They're going to stay a month longer to make up for it."

"Well, I think we should all have a barbecue at the ranch," Nancy says. "The family hasn't all gotten together in too long."

"I'm always game for that," Noah says. "As long as you make your apple pie for dessert."

"I think something can be arranged." Nancy turns to me, flashing me a bright smile. "You should come, too."

"Oh, but it's a family—"

"I'll bring her," Noah says, and that seems to be the end of that. We say our goodbyes and drive back to the sanctuary. "Do you want me to drop you at the house?"

"No, I want to see what happens next," I reply, excited to see Noah in action. Something tells me if I was attracted to him before, watching him work will be fascinating.

It's late enough in the day that all of the summer volunteers have left, but a woman and a man meet us, both anxious to help Noah get the owlets off the truck and inside.

"This is Veronica and Justin," Noah says.

"Call me Roni," Veronica says with a smile. "And nice to meet you."

"I'm Fallon," I reply, following them into a building behind the main office where there are stainless steel tables and all kinds of equipment that is lost on me. "And I don't want to get in the way."

"You're not in the way," Noah says as he and the others take the babies out of the carrier one at a time. They put a tag around an ankle of each, check them over, then Justin moves them to another area to hand-feed them.

"What is he feeding them?" I ask.

"Do you get squeamish?" Justin asks.

"Not usually." My voice is full of caution, but Justin waves me over, and I watch as he feeds the babies mealworms. The owlets are so dang cute, opening their mouths as wide as they can, reaching up for their dinner.

"They're hungry little fellas," Justin says.

"They look like little balls of cotton with heads," I say and laugh. "They're so cute."

"That cotton will turn into feathers," Justin says. "Here, do you want to feed them?"

"Can I?"

"Sure." He passes me the tweezers he's been using to grip the worms, and I feed the babies as Noah brings them to us.

"Oh, you're so cute," I coo to the owlets, who squawk and eat, filling their bellies. "I'm so glad Nancy and Jeff found them."

"Me, too," Roni says. "They would have died overnight."

"But you're going to be okay," I assure them. "Because Noah and Roni and Justin are going to take care of you."

I feel Noah step up behind me, and I look back to smile at him.

"Can I come feed them sometimes?" I ask.

"Whenever you like," he replies. We wash our hands, leaving Roni and Justin to finish. "Do you want to check on your eagle?"

"Yes," I reply immediately. "How is he?"

"Since yesterday? About the same." He chuckles as he leads me to another building and down the line of cages to my eagle's pen. "Oh, but he knows you."

"Yeah, he does. Hi, boy." The eagle watches me intently. "How do you feel today? Still a little rough?"

"He'll be okay. If you want to come feed him tomorrow morning, you can. Unless you have an early class."

"I always have an early class," I murmur. "But I'll come before." I turn to the eagle. "I'll see you tomorrow."

Noah leads me to his truck, and I feel like *I've* been hit by a semi. It's been a long day.

"Thanks for your help," Noah says as he starts the vehicle.

"It was fun." I lean my head back. The drive to his house is less than a minute long, but my eyes are heavy. I didn't get as much sleep last night as I'm used to, and after this day, I'm exhausted.

"Are you asleep?"

My eyes blink open, surprised to be parked at Noah's house with him standing in the open passenger door, leaning over me to lift me into his arms.

"I can walk," I offer.

"No need." He kicks the door shut and kisses my forehead as he carries me up the porch steps and inside. "You're wrecked, Fal."

"No one's ever called me that before," I say with a sleepy sigh. "But I kind of like it."

"Tell me if you don't," he says and lowers me to my bed.

"I'm not shy," I assure him and yawn widely. "But I'm suddenly *so* tired."

"Get some rest." He kisses my forehead again, and I sigh. I'm getting way too used to the forehead kisses that Noah likes to hand out. "I'll be here if you need anything."

I can't keep my eyes open. So, I let sleep pull me under.

Chapter Five

~Noah~

The sun isn't up yet. It's five in the morning, and I'm shuffling around the kitchen, careful not to make too much noise and wake Fallon. I place my mug under the Keurig, and as my coffee brews, I pull the new tea I bought for my houseguest out of the cabinet and set it on the counter next to an electric hot water kettle.

I take my black coffee out onto the back deck and sit on one of the old chairs that have been here for as long as I can remember. All of the furniture in the house is mine, but my parents left their outside things, not needing them in Arizona.

The old chairs are solid, only needing new cushions every few years.

The woods beyond the house, where the bear roamed off to yesterday, are dark, but the sky is purple with the beginnings of the sunrise.

Stars still wink in the sky, and the moon gets ready to set behind me.

Fallon never stirred after I tucked her into bed. She was clearly exhausted. She had a busy few days, with losing her home and moving in here, and everything else that happened. Of course, she was tired.

I wanted to lie with her, to lose myself in her and soak her in, but only a jerk goes where he's not invited. And despite our fun time on my couch yesterday, I'm not invited.

Not yet.

The sliding door behind me opens, and the woman who's occupied most of my thoughts for days pads out onto the deck, barefoot.

"Do you mind if I join you?"

I glance over and smile. Fallon's still in her shorts and tank from yesterday, but she's holding a steaming mug of tea.

"I don't mind at all," I reply softly as she sits in the chair next to mine, tugs her feet up under her the way she always does, and quietly sips from her cup.

We sit in silence for long minutes, listening to the crickets and watching the sky wake up, a riot of orange and purple now, changing by the second as the sun creeps closer and closer to the tops of the mountains in the distance.

"I don't think I've ever seen a place more beautiful than this," she whispers, taking in the show. "And you got to grow up here."

I grin and sip my coffee. "I didn't appreciate it as much as I do now."

Our voices are hushed as if to talk too loudly would wake up the world, and we want to keep it just for us.

"Did it always look like this?"

"Yes." I sigh, stretching my legs out in front of me and enjoying the cool air. "Are you too cold?"

"No, it's nice. It'll get hot again this afternoon."

I nod and sip my coffee. She's not wrong. One thing I love about living in the mountains is even though it does get hot during the day, we cool down nicely at night.

"When I was a kid, we had horses out here," I begin, picturing the way it looked when I was a boy. "We were a much smaller version of the Lazy K. My dad didn't want the responsibility of a big ranch like that and didn't love living out there the way Jeff does. So, when he decided to settle in Cunningham Falls, he and my mom bought this property where he was still out of town, could have a few animals, but not the rough, working-ranch life."

"What did you have besides horses?" Fallon rests her chin on her knees, watching me instead of the sunrise. I can suddenly picture doing this with her every morning for years, which is completely new to me, and not unsettling, so I set it aside and focus on her question.

"Chickens," I reply. "And I got to collect eggs every morning before school. I hated it in the winter."

"I've never had farm-fresh eggs."

My gaze whips to hers in surprise. "I'll get some from Nancy for you. They're delicious. We always had a dog and some cats running around. Over where the sanctuary is now, there used to be a big barn with some equipment, but Dad sold the equipment, and I remodeled the barn to be the flying building. It's the tall, brown building in the back."

As if she's hanging on every word, her gaze follows my hand as I point out the things I mention.

"Would you ever want horses again?"

"No," I reply immediately. "I love to ride, but they're a lot of work, and I have too much to do at the sanctuary."

"Makes sense," she murmurs. "No dogs or cats now, I see."

"There is a cat that roams around the sanctuary. A resident cat, I guess. We named him Shithead."

She snorts.

"And I had a dog until a couple of years ago. He passed away, and I haven't thought about getting another, but I might be close to ready."

"I've never had a pet," she says, surprising me.

"Nothing? Not even a hamster?"

"No." She sips her tea, and I wait. I know she doesn't give up information easily, but I *want* to know more, and I'm learning that it just takes a little time.

I set my empty mug aside and lean back, enjoying the view of the sunrise and the beautiful woman beside me.

"I lived in the city," she begins, and I feel my lips twitch. Yeah, it just takes a little time. "And having a dog would have been a pain because we didn't have a backyard, and I wasn't allowed to walk the neighborhood alone."

So, she lived in a rough neighborhood.

"My parents, well, they weren't really around much. I never met my father, and before you say you're sorry, don't be. From what I've heard, he was no prize. My mom was in and out here and there, but she never stuck around for long. The last I heard, she was living in Texas somewhere with a guy. I honestly don't care.

"My grandma raised me, and I was close to her. We were a team. But there wasn't room in the budget for a cat or anything, and I never really craved one. I guess you don't miss what you've never had."

She clears her throat and looks over at me. "Go on."

"That's it, really."

I doubt that.

"How long has your grandmother been gone?"

"Oh, gosh, six years I guess." She sets her empty mug aside and wraps her arms around her legs, holding them close to her chest.

The woman is fucking flexible.

"And you were an accountant?"

A smile tips the corners of her lips. "Yeah. I hated it. I went to school for it because I figured I'd always have a stable job that way, and I was right. I worked in a good firm in Chicago, and by the time I left, I was the head of my department."

"What happened?"

"Grandma died," she says simply. "And when I returned to work after settling her affairs, I couldn't help but think it wasn't what she would have wanted for me. To go to a job every day that was sucking the life out of me. She did that her whole life, and I knew she didn't want it for me.

"So, I handed in my resignation, sold most of my things, including Grandma's apartment, and I've been a nomad ever since. I have a bucket list of places I'd like to live, and I stay for as long as I'm happy, and then I move on. I studied yoga, fell in love with it, and thankfully, I'm able to teach wherever I go."

"So, Cunningham Falls isn't necessarily where you plan to set down roots."

It's not a question, and for reasons I'm not ready to examine, it pisses me off.

"I hadn't planned to, no."

"But?"

"But." She sighs deeply, just as the sun peeks over the top of the mountain. "I've been here the longest, and when I think of moving on, it makes me sad."

"So don't move on. At least, not yet."

"I don't plan to," she replies with a soft smile, then sobers. "Is this odd to you, that we're starting something while I'm staying with you? Should we back off and wait for my living arrangements to get figured out? Because we *are* starting something. I can't be the only one to feel it."

"You're not," I assure her. "We're starting something. And we're not backing off. I'll take things as slow as you like, Fallon. We're in no hurry, and I'm not a jerk who thinks you need to sleep with me if you're staying here. So, if you made your move yesterday because of that—"

"No." Her voice is firm, maybe leaning toward mad. "I made my move because I find you attractive and I wanted to climb on top of you."

"Understood." I grin. "And appreciated."

"I think you're the kind of guy who doesn't pull any punches," she continues.

"I'd say you're right."

"And I'm the same. I want to make sure we're on the same page."

"Do you want to back off?" I ask and watch her face closely, the way her plump lips pucker, and frown lines form between her brows as she thinks it over.

I appreciate that she's *thinking* and not just reacting.

God, she's fantastic.

"No," she says, shaking her head. "I don't. I'm fine with where we are."

"Good." I stand and hold out my hand for hers. "Now, let's go feed your eagle."

"Perfect."

* * * *

"I can't believe you've never been to the farmer's market," Fallon says later that evening as she drives us both into town in her Jeep. We have to go to the edge of town where Frontier Park is. "I mean, I'm new here, and I go all the time."

"I just never had a reason to," I reply and grin, enjoying the way the wind brushes the loose strands of hair that fell out of her ponytail over her cheek.

"You're going to love it," she assures me.

She's sexy as fuck driving this Jeep, in another pair of short, denim shorts and a pink tank that hugs her curves. It seems this is Fallon's summer outfit of choice, and I'm not complaining in the least.

She's lean and tanned, her eyes covered in big sunglasses. She taps her fingers on the steering wheel as Taylor Swift sings about shaking it off.

"I like your Jeep."

She grins. "Me, too. It'll take me anywhere I want to go, it's comfortable, and it's kind of badass."

"Like the woman driving it," I reply.

"Damn right."

She pulls into a busy parking lot and has to circle a couple of times before she nabs a space that was just vacated.

"Busy place." I hop out of the Jeep, no door to slam, and meet her on the sidewalk. She slips her hand into mine as if it's the most natural thing in the world to do, and we stand to survey the scene.

There is a line of food trucks at the opposite end of the parking lot. Lines of tables covered with awnings are on the grass, and a mobile stage is set up in the middle with a band playing some country music.

"So, to the right is all the produce," she says, pointing it out and giving me the lay of the land. "The rest of the tables are full of crafts, non-perishable foods, art...you get the idea."

"Gotcha." I nod, but I'm not looking around the park, I'm watching her face. She pushes her glasses up on her head and smiles at someone who walks by, loaded down with vegetables.

"We can grab dinner when we're done," she suggests.

"I love me some food truck food," I say and pat my stomach, making her laugh. "Where do you want to start?"

"I like to go and pick out some produce, and then I wander through the rest. Oh! I almost forgot my basket."

She hurries to the back of the Jeep and returns with a big canvas basket that's covered in red flowers.

"Are you planning to buy all of the produce here?" I ask, eyeing the size of the basket hooked on her elbow.

"I usually get quite a bit," she says with a nod. "I prefer to buy it here rather than the grocery store. It's fresher, and I'm supporting local businesses."

"And you've never had farm-fresh eggs?"

She sighs in exasperation and drops her glasses back onto her nose. "Are you going to judge me or help me shop?"

"Maybe both," I say and shrug, following her down the long line of vendors selling their wares.

"Do you mind if I cook some dinners this week?" she asks as she feels the weight of a cantaloupe, smells it, and then places it into her basket. I take it from her.

"If you start cooking for me, I might not ever let you move out."

She smiles up at me, and I want to kiss her right there in front of the whole town. Her teeth are bright against her tanned skin, and she looks happy and carefree.

I feel the same when I'm with her.

"So, that's a yes, then," she says and glances over some lettuce, but it must not meet her standards because she moves on without buying any.

"Hey, Noah."

I glance up, surprised to see Ty Sullivan. He has a baby on his hip and another in an infant carrier against his stomach.

He looks damn happy.

"Hey, man," I say and shake his hand. "I didn't know you were a farmer's market man."

"We live over the bridge," he says, gesturing to the other side of the park. "So, we usually bring the kids and walk over. You must be Fallon?"

She smiles and offers her hand. "Okay, I don't know how you know that, but you're right."

"My wife, Lauren, takes your classes, and she's pointed you out to me before."

"Oh, wonderful," Fallon says, looking around. "Is Lauren here?"

"She and Jillian King are off checking out a new artist."

"Well, I'll say hi if I run into her," Fallon says and turns her attention to the little girl shyly holding onto Ty's neck. "Aren't you just the prettiest little thing?"

"She's tired," Ty says when the baby hides her face. "It was good to see you, Noah. See you out at the Lazy K this weekend? I've been told there's a BBQ happening."

"We'll see you there," I confirm, and we say our goodbyes.

"You all know each other," Fallon says as we wander through the maze of people. "It's so interesting."

"Small town," I reply with a smile. "So, Josh and Zack are my cousins. They're about five years older than me, and Ty has been their best friend since they were small kids."

"Gotcha," she says and nods but then laughs. "I think. Everyone should wear nametags."

"You'll catch on," I assure her. "You already know the girls."

"True," she says.

We end up filling the basket full of fruits and vegetables and even some meats from the butcher. A Lady Antebellum song plays as we wander through the arts and crafts, saying hello to people we know, and politely nodding to those we don't—which isn't many.

Finally, with our arms full, we reach the sidewalk where the Jeep is parked.

"I usually just put this in the backseat and then walk down for some dinner," Fallon says, but I motion for her to stay on the sidewalk.

"I've got it. Wait here."

She nods, and I walk the block or so to the Jeep and set her finds in the backseat, then move things around so it's all in the shade.

It won't get stolen, but we also don't want it to bake in the sun.

When I walk back toward Fallon, I see she's chatting with a man I don't recognize. Her hands are in her back pockets, pushing her breasts forward, and she's smiling sweetly at him.

I don't like it. I don't like it at all.

"I don't think we've met," I say in greeting, my voice even. "I'm Noah King."

"Dude," he says with a chuckle. "It's Sam. Waters."

"How did I not recognize you?" I ask, shaking my head and grasping his hand. Sam grew up here, the same as the rest of us. He was older than Gray and me, but I've known him my whole life. "You're bigger."

"Rude," Fallon says with a smirk.

"As in muscles, smartass," I reply and tug on her ponytail.

"I've been working out," Sam says with a shrug. "And I've been taking some yoga classes from Fallon."

"So, that's how you know each other."

"He's a good student," Fallon says and pats Sam's arm. My hackles rise again. Sam looks at her like she hung the fucking moon.

"Are you still a paramedic?" I ask.

Because you might need to call a friend if you keep looking at her like that.

"Yeah, and I'm on the fire department, too," he says. "It was time to up my game with my fitness if I'm going to be rescuing people from burning buildings and all that."

"Congratulations," I reply. "That's great. How's Evan?"

"Who's Evan?" Fallon asks.

"My brother," Sam replies. "He's great. I'll tell him you said hi."

"Sounds good, man." I turn to Fallon and slip my hand into hers. "Shall we go get that dinner?"

"Yes, I'm starving," she says and turns to Sam. "See you in class."

"See you," Sam says and waves before walking into the crowd of the market.

"What are you in the mood for?" she asks as we approach the line of trucks. "I have to say, this may be a small town, but this is an impressive choice of food. Italian, Mexican, burgers—"

"Are you fucking Sam?" I blurt, and we stop on the sidewalk, twenty yards from the food.

Without a word, Fallon drops my hand and faces me head-on, her hands on her slim hips, her face tipped up to look at me. She pushes her glasses up on her head again, and her green eyes are hot with anger.

"Did you just ask me that?"

"I did."

I shove my hands into my pockets, unwilling to back down.

Fallon steps closer, narrowing her eyes. She's a pint-sized ball of fury.

It's fascinating and not a little arousing.

"You know what, Noah? Fuck you. You don't get to ask me that, in public, after the past few days we've had together. If you have to ask, you're not the kind of man I want to be involved with."

And with that, she stomps away and gets in the pizza line.

I'm left on the sidewalk, feeling ashamed and turned on all at the same time. I take a deep breath and join her.

"I owe you a hell of an apology."

"Huge," she agrees and steps forward when the line moves. "Jealousy isn't sexy, Noah. And, honestly, I thought you were better than that."

"Me, too," I reply and rub the back of my neck in agitation. "It doesn't feel good."

"I'm allowed to know people," she continues, her voice soft so she doesn't get attention from the people around us. "Men people. And if you don't like that, we can stop this right now."

"No," I say, shaking my head. "I'm a dick."

"Big time."

"I should be punished."

"Do you have a bullwhip?"

I stare down at her in surprise. "You're violent."

Her lips quirk into an evil smile. "I'm totally kidding."

"Uh-huh." We reach the front of the line, and she orders a slice of vegetarian pizza and an order of breadsticks. I order two slices of pepperoni and more breadsticks.

To go.

"Let's go home to eat," I say after I pay and we move to the end of the truck to gather our food. "I'd rather not be whipped in public."

Chapter Six

~Fallon~

I'm pissed.

Beyond pissed.

I'm also hurt and frustrated and concerned that this side of Noah that he showed me at the market will become a habit. Because I won't tolerate that.

No way, no how.

After eating in silence, I toss my pizza containers in the garbage, and start cleaning the vegetables and fruits I bought, putting them away in the fridge. Just as I'm finishing up, Noah comes into the kitchen.

"I'm going for a walk," I announce, not looking him in the face. I need some exercise to clear my head.

"Mind if I join you?" he asks softly.

I turn away and cringe. I'm not sure that I want his company right now, but maybe this will be a good time to have a frank conversation with him.

"I don't mind," I reply. Noah grabs a can of bear spray, hooks it to his belt, and we set off down the gravel road.

He's quiet as we walk along, watching birds fly and listening to the sounds the woods make. It used to scare me, but now I find it peaceful.

I take a deep breath, already starting to feel better.

"You're quiet," he says softly.

"I'm not really sure what to say," I admit. "Here's the thing. You didn't ask me if I had feelings for Sam or if I had ever dated him. You asked me if I'd *fucked* him. No, check that, you asked if I *am* fucking him."

I shake my head, getting mad all over again.

"So, I have some concerns about that. Either you assume I'm a slut who will flirt with and come on to a man—you—while simultaneously pursuing Sam, or you're a controlling dick, and this is the first sign of that. Because, frankly, my grandma always said, when someone shows you who they are, believe them."

"She was a smart woman," Noah says with a sigh.

"Very," I agree and nod. "And neither of those two options sits well with me, Noah."

"They don't sit well with me, either," he says, shaking his head. "And I'll apologize again. I was wrong to ask you that, and I don't believe you're a slut. I'm also not a dick who tries to control women."

"Then what the hell?"

"I saw him smiling at you, and you smiling back, and I instantly saw green."

"Yeah, I can see where smiling must be quite threatening," I reply, rolling my eyes.

"Here's the truth of it." He stops and faces me, his hands on his hips. He looks ashamed, his eyes frustrated. "I've never felt the need to claim someone before. I know it sounds barbaric, but there's no other way to describe it. It was instinctual. And *wrong.*"

"You don't have a reason to feel insecure," I point out.

"No, I don't," he agrees. "And I should have taken a deep breath and thought about my question before I asked it."

"Absolutely. I'll clear the air right here about Sam, and anyone else in town. I'm not sleeping with them. I'm not dating. I do have acquaintances, both male and female, who I smile at when I see in public."

"Point taken," Noah replies.

"I'm not the kind of girl who sticks around when a man is a dick, just because he's also nice to me sometimes. That's not me. Now, or ever."

"I'm damn happy to hear that," he says, and I can see that he means it. "I'm not the man to tell you that you can't be yourself. I like *you.* A lot. I'm attracted to you. Hell, I can barely keep my hands off you. But I also enjoy being with you, having a conversation. I'm embarrassed that I acted that way, and I'm telling you, I'm not that guy."

I watch him for a moment, his eyes holding mine, and I believe him.

So I nod and take a long, deep breath.

"Thank you," I say at last. Then I turn back toward the house. The walk back is so much different.

Comfortable.

"So," he begins, "pistachio ice cream, green, pinot gris, tea, and no dick behavior."

"That's a good start."

He takes my hand in his, pulls it to his lips, and kisses my knuckles.

Every time he touches me, it's like electricity shooting through my nerves straight to my core. My gut tells me he's telling the truth.

My instincts haven't steered me wrong yet.

* * * *

When we return to the house, Noah gets a call from Roni, asking him to come over to the sanctuary to help with something. He hurries over there, and I stay at the house.

I'm used to having alone-time. A lot of it. And while I enjoy Noah and his company, having an hour or so alone sounds good.

So, I do some laundry and take a shower, and then sit on the back deck, eating pistachio ice cream and watching the mountains turn pink while the sun sets behind me.

I still can't believe that it's almost ten in the evening, and the sun is just now setting.

I think that's one of the reasons I've stayed in Montana so long, the long days in the summer. It's hot outside, but I can already feel the cool night creeping in, taking the edge off.

I glance to my right and see Noah walking back to the house down the road that connects it to his sanctuary. He's walking at a fast pace, but with legs as long as his, that's his normal gait.

He slows way down when he walks with me.

I take a bite of my ice cream, watching as he approaches. He sits on the steps next to me.

"Everything okay over there?" I ask.

"Oh, yeah," he says with a nod and a glance at my spoon. "Can I have a bite?"

I cock a brow, but load the spoon and offer it to him. He smiles, nudges the ice cream aside, and lowers his lips to mine, kissing me deeply, sinking into me.

"Delicious," he says when he pulls away.

I drop the spoon into the almost-empty tub, set it aside, and straddle him, ignoring the press of the wooden deck on my knees as I fuse my lips to his. His hands roam up and down my back and then move to my ass. With a firm grip, he lifts me easily, and I wrap my legs around his waist as he carries me into the house and through the living area to his bedroom.

"If this isn't where you want to take this," he murmurs as he buries his face in my throat, "I need to know right now."

"We've been heading here for a while." I reply and laugh when he dumps me on the bed. I bounce twice and scoot back, watching him shuck his jeans and T-shirt, unabashedly checking out the view before me.

Tanned skin. Long, lean muscles. Abs for days, and a smirk on maybe the most handsome face I've ever seen.

Yeah. We're doing this.

"You're still dressed," he says, leaning over to kiss his way up my leg. He reaches the hem of my shorts and nudges his way under it with his nose, sending shivers over my skin. "And so soft."

I reach to unfasten my button, but he stops me, popping it open with his teeth and then peeling the shorts down my legs and tossing them over his shoulder.

His brown eyes whip up to mine.

"Do you always go commando?"

"Usually," I say as if it's no big deal. He swallows hard.

"Jesus, I'll never be able to keep myself from stripping you naked," he mutters, his eyes roaming over the bottom half of my body. "No bra, no panties."

"My breasts aren't impressive enough to warrant a bra."

"Your breasts are fucking impressive," he growls, pulling my tank over my head and tossing it in the same direction of my shorts, then latching on to a nipple and sucking hard.

My hips come up off the bed, but he spreads my legs and drags his fingertips up and down my inner thighs.

My God, the way he touches me sends me into crazytown.

"They're so damn responsive," he murmurs, plucking a nipple with his lips and then moving on to the other one. His fingers dance over the lips of my labia, and my hips rotate. "Your body is amazing."

I smile and bury my fingers in his soft, dark hair. I want him *now,* but I also want to take our time, enjoying every touch, kiss, and amazing sensation.

Noah kisses his way down my belly and spreads my legs wider, seemingly enjoying the view.

"So pink," he says with a grin before lapping his tongue through my folds, his eyes boldly on mine. "And delicious."

My God, he's going to kill me.

I fist the bedsheets and arch my back, and then he's suddenly gone, riffling through his bedside drawer and coming back with a sealed box of condoms.

"I was optimistic," he says with a grin, opening the box and ripping a condom free from the others. He tears it open with his teeth.

"I don't get to repay the favor?" I ask before he rolls it over his cock. He stops short.

"Sweetheart, if you do that now, I'll embarrass myself." His smile is rueful as he finishes rolling on the condom, and then he covers me once more, kissing me deeply. "I want to take this slow."

"If you go any slower, you'll kill me."

He smiles against my lips as his cock rests over my pussy.

"Slow next time?" he asks.

"Deal."

And with that, he rears back and eases his way inside me slowly, taking care not to hurt me. He's big, but I'm turned on and ready for him.

"So slick," he mutters, gritting his teeth. "And damn snug."

I raise my knees, urging him to go deeper, and he kisses my calves, then rests them on his shoulders and moves into a rhythm, in and out at a steady pace, not too fast but urging us to both chase our orgasms.

I don't have any choice. The orgasm moves through me, from my spine and up to my neck, almost choking me with sensation and emotion that I don't think I've ever felt in my life.

"Christ, I'm coming," he mutters and groans with his own release. He pants and watches me closely. "Are you okay?"

"Aside from my body humming from head to toe and the fact that I can't feel my face, I'm doing great."

He smiles and kisses my lips, then eases off me and pads into the bathroom to dispose of the condom. He returns with a warm, wet towel.

He cleans us up, then joins me under the covers, pulling me to him.

"I didn't take you for a snuggler," I admit, enjoying the way his chest feels under my cheek.

"Never have been," he says and kisses the top of my head. "But I like the way you feel. Sleep here tonight."

I frown into the darkness but don't move away.

Am I ready for a sleepover?

I yawn and tangle my leg with his, content to stay here through the night. Noah's breathing becomes slow and steady with sleep, and he lulls me there right behind him.

* * * *

My phone is ringing.

I frown, open one eye, and survey the area. I'm in Noah's room, under crisp, white sheets. Sunlight streams through the window, telling me it's later than usual for me.

I turn to Noah's side of the bed, but he's gone.

"Hello?" I say into the phone.

"Good morning," Claire says cheerfully. "Are you at work?"

"No." I frown and check the time. Seven-thirty. I really overslept. "I don't have class until noon today."

"Cool," she replies and crunches on something in my ear. "So, how are things?"

"Fine." I smile at Noah as he walks into the room, wearing navy blue lounge pants and nothing else, carrying a mug of coffee and a cup of tea. He sets them both on the side table, pulls off his pants, and slips under the covers with me.

"You're not talkative this morning," Claire says as Noah buries his face against my throat, tickling me.

"I just woke up," I reply and bite my lip, trying not to giggle.

"Why do you sound weird?"

"I don't." I frown at Noah and shake my head, but he just grins and kisses my nipple. "What's going on with you?"

"Oh, you know, same ol', same ol'. Remember Henry from HR?"

"The old geezer who used to piss you off all the time?" I ask and then gasp when Noah sinks a finger inside me.

"No, that's Harry. Henry was the younger one they hired right before you quit."

"Oh." I bite my lip again, surprised it's not bleeding. "Right. Him."

"So, he took me out on a date last night."

"Yeah?" I slap at Noah's arm, but he ignores me, continuing to play with me. "How'd that go?"

"Are you having sex?" she asks out of the blue, and Noah smiles widely, nodding his head emphatically.

"No." It's not a lie. I scowl, trying to warn him to stop, but he just shrugs and nudges his shoulders between my legs.

Shit, I won't be able to pull this off.

"Forget Henry," Claire says with a laugh. "Who is he?"

"Noah," I say and glare at the man who's just sealed his lips over my clit. "And he's being naughty right now."

"Good for Noah. I love the happiness I hear in your voice, but can we keep this rated PG?"

Noah says loudly enough for Claire to hear, "No, she has to go now."

"Call me later," Claire says with a laugh. "I'll want to hear all about him."

"Okay. Bye." I click off and giggle. "That wasn't nice, Noah."

"No?"

I shake my head.

"This isn't nice?" He licks me the way he did last night, but instead of leaving to grab a condom, he keeps going, tickling the edges of my core and the crease where my legs meet my center, making my toes curl.

"Oh, that does feel nice." I sigh.

"And what about this?" His tongue follows his fingertips, and I sigh again in bliss.

"Yeah."

He flips me over easily, brushes my hair out of his way, and kisses the back of my neck, then down my spine to my ass.

"You have a great butt," he says before he nibbles on one cheek. "It fits in my hands perfectly."

"So glad you approve," I reply and laugh, and then sigh yet again when his fingertips dip into the promised land, making my eyes cross. "God, you're good with your hands."

"Just my hands?"

I feel him reach for a condom and grin in anticipation.

"Other parts, too."

He holds my legs together and straddles them, then spreads my cheeks apart and slips his cock inside me, making me gasp.

"Holy shit," I mutter.

"Too much?" He stills, waiting for my answer.

"No. Just—" I lick my lips and take a deep breath. "You feel huge in this position."

He leans in and presses his lips to my ear. "That's the goal. If it's too much, just say so."

I nod, and he begins to move.

I won't last long like this. It's overwhelming, the size of him. The way he fills me.

The way he makes me feel.

Vulnerable and safe all at the same time.

Sex with Noah is not just a physical thing.

"How's that?"

I can't form words.

"Fal," he says softly but maintains his rhythm. "Tell me."

"So good," I gasp. "So, so good."

I feel him grin before he sits up on his knees, bracing himself on the headboard with one hand and my hip with the other. The next thing I know, my orgasm is back, wrapping its way around my torso, shooting through my fingers and toes.

"Jesus," he says when he can breathe again. The routine is the same from last night, dispose of the condom and clean us up, and then he's smiling down at me. "Your tea is cold. I have to go brew you a fresh cup."

I drag my fingertips down his cheek, enjoying the way the stubble feels against my short nails.

"I can brew my tea," I offer. "And your coffee if you like."

He kisses my forehead in that way that makes me soften. "Thank you."

"I'll even cook breakfast."

"I won't complain." He grins, waggles his eyebrows, and springs from the bed, pulling on clothes. "I don't remember the last time I slept this late."

"Me either," I admit. "Are you late for work?"

"Nah, they've got it handled. I told them I'd be hit and miss today anyway. What about you?"

"I don't work until noon." I pad from the bed, out into the hallway, and walk naked to my room. Noah follows. "What do you have going on today?"

"My parents are coming in."

I stop, pull my tank over my head, and stare at him. "Do they need this room?"

"No, they usually stay with Jeff and Nancy." He smiles and leans on the doorframe as he watches me get dressed. "Dad likes to play ranch hand for a few months, and Mom and Nancy are besties."

"Did you just say *besties*?"

"What? They are."

I laugh and shake my head. "Who's your *bestie*?"

"Gray," he says immediately. "And Max. What about you?"

I frown and pull on my yoga pants, thinking about it. "Claire is my closest friend," I say at last. "And Penny."

Noah just nods and walks to me, pulling me in for a hug.

"I forgot to say good morning."

"No." I rest my cheek against his hard chest and listen to his heartbeat. "You said it very well, if I remember correctly."

Chapter Seven

~Noah~

"Get in," Gray says as he pulls up beside me. I'm in the yard, and was pulling some weeds in the flowerbed while waiting for my brother to come and pick me up.

If Mom comes to the house and sees the overgrowth, I'll get an earful.

"How's it going?" I ask as he drives his truck away from my place.

"Right as rain," he says, a shit-eating grin all over his face. Gray is only a year older than I am, and we look alike. "Life's good when you're in love, brother of mine."

"I'm happy that you're happy, but you're kind of mushy," I reply and grin. I love harassing him. "Should we put some Celine Dion on the radio?"

"Eff you," he says with a laugh. "You're just jealous."

"Nah," I say, shaking my head. "How is Autumn?"

My brother met his fiancée, Autumn, this past winter while skiing on Whitetail Mountain. He literally plowed right into her, and for reasons that still escape me, she fell in love with him.

"She's gorgeous," he replies immediately. "And doing well. She's visiting her brother and Skylar in Billings."

I nod as he pulls onto the highway. "Will she be back in time for the BBQ at the ranch on Sunday?"

"Should be," he replies and tells me all about Autumn and the wedding plans for next summer. I sit back and listen, happy that he's so excited. I like Autumn. She's a beautiful redhead, originally from Scotland. Her brother, Killian, is a successful record producer, and his fiancée Skylar is an international superstar.

"I'm bringing Fallon," I inform him and earn a stunned glance from Gray.

"You're bringing a woman over to meet the family? This is a first."

I shrug and look out the passenger window as we drive out to the Lazy K. "Never met anyone worth introducing to them before."

Gray's quiet for a long moment, so I look over and see that he's watching the road, frowning.

"What? You don't like her?"

"I met her once," he reminds me. "And she seemed nice. If you like her enough to bring her to a family thing, you must really like her."

"I do," I admit. "She's…different. And before you flip me any shit, just remember you're engaged and practically singing Celine Dion songs."

"Hey, I think it's great," he says and smiles. "Good for you."

He pulls off the highway onto the Lazy K Ranch road. The ranch has changed so much since we were kids, with new homes built and the addition of more livestock since Zack and Josh started running it together.

We spent so much time out here as kids, running wild in the woods, playing in the creeks, and exploring every nook and cranny of the place.

It's our second home.

Gray drives past what we call the Big House, where Zack and Jillian live with their kids, and turn before we reach Josh and Cara's place.

The road takes us to the other side of a huge pasture where Jeff and Nancy built a cottage a few years ago.

We have a surprise for our parents today.

Mom and Dad's SUV is parked in front of the cottage, still loaded down with their things.

"Think they'll be surprised?" I ask Gray as he parks.

"Mom's gonna cry like a baby." He grins at me as he opens his door. "It's going to be awesome."

We don't have to knock on the door before it flings open, and Mom runs out, her arms flung wide, and a huge smile on her beautiful face.

"My boys!" she cries and pulls us both in for hugs. "My sweet little boys."

"Not so little these days," Dad says with a grin, waiting his turn to hug us and slap us on the back. "Taller than me."

"They'll always be my little boys," Mom says and wipes a tear from her eye. She's a petite woman with blond hair and a sweet smile. Dad's tall and lean just like Jeff and the rest of us boys.

The King genes are strong.

"I guess we should start unloading this car," Dad says, and Gray and I look at Jeff and Nancy, unable to control our grins.

"Well, you're not staying here," Jeff says with a sigh. "Nan and I just don't have the space."

Mom frowns at Nancy. "Why didn't you say? We can rent a house in town."

"That won't be necessary," Gray says, shaking his head. "I think we have the perfect spot for you."

Nancy smiles and claps her hands, unable to keep a secret for long.

"Come on, I can't stand it any longer," she says and takes Mom's hand in hers. "We have a surprise."

"What's going on?" Dad asks, a frown clear on his face.

"Get in your car and follow us," I suggest.

"Excellent idea," Jeff says, climbing into the backseat of Mom and Dad's SUV. "Let's go, boys."

Gray and I make our way down the fresh road and around a bend where another cottage has just been built.

You can't see it from Jeff and Nancy's, but it's only a five-minute walk away.

We get out of the truck as Dad pulls in behind us and they step out of the car, shock all over their faces.

"We did a thing," Gray says, gesturing to the white cabin in the woods. It's small, with a covered front porch, and black shutters. "This way, you have your own place to come in the summers."

"Boys," Mom whispers, covering her mouth with a shaking hand. "This is too much."

"It's your home, too," Jeff says, clapping his brother on the shoulder. "You have as much of a claim to it as I do."

"We both know that's bullshit," Dad says but looks at Jeff with a smile. "But thank you."

"We have all the space in the world," Nancy says, looping her arm through Mom's. "And just wait until you see what Gray did inside."

"Gray built it?" Mom asks.

"Along with Zack," Gray says and nods. "It's not fancy—"

"It's perfect," Dad says, his voice rough, as they step inside ahead of us.

There's an open living space with a small sitting room, dining area, and a white kitchen with a little island.

To the right, a hallway leads to two bedrooms and two bathrooms.

"Oh, boys," Mom says, looking everywhere at once. "This is just fabulous."

"And you'll still be close," Nancy reminds her.

"It seems a shame that it'll sit here empty most of the year," Dad says, taking it all in.

"We have plenty of people around to check in on it," Jeff reassures, waving him off. "And this little piece of land was sitting empty anyway."

"Thank you," Mom says, giving us all hugs. "It's just so beautiful."

"You're welcome," Gray replies. "Now that you've seen this, you should ask Noah about his girlfriend."

I glare at my brother in surprise just as Mom turns to me with a gasp.

"What?" she demands. "Where is she?"

"Not here," I reply. "And I've just barely started seeing her."

"Oh, I really like her," Nancy says, making Mom scowl. "She's just the sweetest thing. And so pretty, too."

"Nancy's met her, and I haven't even *heard* of her?"

I glare at my brother. "I'm going to smother you in your sleep."

Gray just laughs as Nancy tells Mom all about Fallon while Dad and Jeff step out the back door to the patio that butts up to the woods.

"When do I get to meet her?" Mom demands.

"Sunday," I say, praying that bringing Fallon around my big, loud family doesn't scare her off. "She'll come to the party on Sunday."

"She'd better," Mom says, giving me the *mom look*. "And where is Autumn?"

I turn to Gray with a grin. "Yeah, where's *Autumn*?"

"In Billings, but she'll be here on Sunday, too."

"Good." Mom turns to Nancy. "My boys have girls, Nan. When did we get this old?"

"I have a million grandkids," Nancy reminds her. "Trust me, you're preaching to the choir."

* * * *

"You are beautiful," I say to Fallon. It's early evening, and I've decided to take her out on a date. We may be living together, but this is still new, and she deserves to be courted.

She grins over at me and reaches for my hand, giving it a squeeze. I'm driving us to town for dinner and a movie. It's casual, but that seems to be our jam.

"Do you mind swinging by my place?" she asks. "I'd like to see how they're coming along."

"No problem." I turn toward her rental. The windows in my SUV are rolled down, and we're enjoying the warm air. One thing about Fallon, she'd rather have the fresh air than the A/C, and I love that, especially this time of year when it's hot outside, and it smells like trees and summer.

Jenna and Christian are walking to their car just as we pull in behind them.

"Good timing," Fallon mutters as she pushes out of my vehicle and smiles at Jenna. "Hey, guys. Is that a *condemned* sign on my door?"

"Yeah," Jenna says with a sigh. "I was about to call you, Fallon. Hi, Noah."

"Hey," I reply and nod at Christian, who nods back. "What's up?"

"Mold," Christian replies. "I'm sorry, Fallon, but they found more leakage in the crawlspace under the house, and a lot of black mold."

"I'm so relieved that ceiling fell in," Jenna adds. "As much of a pain in the ass as it is, it could have saved you from a lot of medical issues. I'm so, *so* sorry."

Fallon plucks at her lip, listening and staring at the house. "Should I find another place? Do *you* have another place for rent, Jenna?"

"It's summer, and I'm full right now," Jenna replies. I can see the distress on her face, she truly feels awful about the situation.

I don't. Fallon can stay with me indefinitely as far as I'm concerned, but I know it's early days yet, and she'd feel more comfortable in her own space.

"I do have a vacation rental," Jenna continues. "It will be empty in about two weeks. You're welcome to take that as soon as it's free."

"Rent-free, of course," Christian adds. "We really feel bad, Fallon."

"It's not your fault," Fallon says and takes a long, deep breath. "I knew it was an older house when I moved in. I'll take you up on that vacation rental when it's available."

"Great," Jenna replies and turns to me. "Does that work for you?"

"Fine with me," I say and slip my hand into Fallon's. "I'm in no hurry to see her go."

"You're a cute couple," Jenna says with a smile. "I like it. A lot. Have you seen Max lately?"

"No, I didn't know if he and Willa were back from their honeymoon."

"They got back a few days ago," Jenna says. "He'd be interested to hear all about the new things happening in your life."

"We don't really gossip like women," I reply, earning a roll of the eyes from Jenna.

"Sure, you don't. That's why all you guys used to go to his place to shoot pool. Just to *not* talk."

"I'll call him," I reply. "Do you need anything from us for now?"

"No." Jenna turns to Fallon. "I really *am* sorry, Fallon."

"Please, don't worry," Fallon replies, pulling Jenna in for a hug. "I'm fine. Just let me know when the other place is ready."

"Will do," Christian says, and we say our goodbyes, pulling away from the house.

"Well, that sucks," she mutters. "I guess it's good that Jenna has another place opening up soon."

I nod and drive us to the other side of town where my favorite BBQ restaurant is. The Back Room has been a community staple in Cunningham Falls for three generations.

"I've never been here," Fallon says when she looks up.

"Then you've never lived." I wink at her and hop out of the vehicle, escorting her inside. We're shown to a booth, and once we've ordered drinks, perused the menu, and ordered food, I watch Fallon, wondering how to lighten her mood. "Whenever I had a birthday when I was a kid, I asked to come here for dinner."

"Really?" She smiles and looks around. It's a rustic, family-owned place. "It smells good."

"Wait until you try the frybread and honey butter." I lick my lips. "It'll change your life."

"That's a bold statement."

I hold up my hands. "I swear it. Life-changing."

Our food is quickly delivered, and my mouth immediately waters. Baby back ribs, baby red potatoes, baked beans, coleslaw, Fallon's chicken, and let's not forget a big slab of frybread with honey butter.

This is heaven on a plate.

"I'll never eat all of this," Fallon says in surprise, and I grin at her.

"I'll eat what you don't, sweetheart."

I take a bite of a rib, deliberately leaving the sauce all over my lips. Fallon looks up and breaks out in a giggle.

"You're a mess," she says.

"What? Do I have something on my face?"

She laughs now, covering her mouth as she chews her coleslaw. "You're ridiculous."

"Delicious," I say, stuffing more food into my mouth, not bothering to wipe my face clean. "BBQ should be messy."

"Okay, caveman, grab some napkins."

I smile and reach for the roll of paper towels on the end of the table, tearing off a handful and wiping my lips. "Better?"

"You'll need a shower when we get home."

"Maybe you should take it with me," I suggest, watching as her green eyes go from full of humor to all-out lust.

"I guess someone has to make sure you get all the sauce off your face."

"Yeah, and you could probably wash my back."

"Suck your cock," she suggests before taking a bite of her bread, and my dick comes to full alert. She's as casual as you please, as if she suggested she'd pass me the soap. "Mm, you were right. This bread is ridiculously amazing."

"Maybe we should skip the date and go right for the shower," I suggest, making her laugh again.

"No way, cowboy. I'm enjoying myself. Thanks, by the way. I know I was a little pissy there for a minute."

"No one can resist BBQ sauce face," I reply and take another bite of my ribs. "And don't sweat it, honey. I'm not in any rush to kick you out, so unless staying at my place is horrible—"

"It's definitely not."

"Then I'd say things are fine. I'm glad you got out of that house before it made you sick."

"Me, too." She bites into her rotisserie chicken and sighs in happiness. "I just feel bad for Jenna. It has to cost a fortune to fix all of that."

"She can afford it," I reply with a shrug. "And it's something you take on when you're a landlord. Things can happen, and you have to be ready for it. I know she plans for things with the hopes she won't have to deal with them."

"Smart," Fallon says. "I wonder if Max and Willa had a fun honeymoon?"

"They toured their way through Europe," I reply with a nod. "I'm sure they had a fantastic time. I didn't know he was home. I'll call him later."

"Willa's a sweetheart," Fallon says. "She's been in my yoga class for at least a year now."

"She's the best," I agree. "I thought Max was an idiot for letting her go when they were in high school."

"What happened there?"

"They dated in school. Max was a year ahead of her and went away to college, but he broke it off before he left. I guess Willa didn't want to go away for school. His best friend back then was Cary Monroe, who was the same age as Max, but he stayed here rather than going off to college. He and Willa ended up together.

"But not long after they married, when Willa was a few weeks from having Alex, Cary died in a skiing accident. Max was with him at the time."

"Oh, that's horrible," Fallon says softly.

"It was a rough time," I agree. "I was away at college, but I came home for the funeral. I felt bad for all of them."

"But they ended up together anyway."

"Yeah, almost a decade later, they found their way back. Max should have made his move years ago, but I suppose he was afraid. I pushed him into asking her out."

"How?" She takes a bite of her beans, watching me avidly. God, I love talking with her.

"I threatened to ask her out myself," I say with a smile. "He didn't like that."

"I'm sure he didn't," she replies. "Good thinking."

"It would have happened eventually. I'm happy for them. It'll be good to see him."

"I remember after their first date, Willa came into yoga and told us all about it. I could see it on her face then, she was completely in love with him."

"Do the women talk about their love lives often in class?"

She laughs and shakes her head. "We're mostly quiet, but she was excited that day, and Jenna wanted to talk about it. If I remember right, Lo and Jillian were there, too, and a few others. You all know each other, so they wanted the scoop."

"You always talk about the people you know as if they're separate from you," I reply thoughtfully. "'*You* all know each other.' You live here too, Fal. You know them."

"I guess I hadn't thought of it like that." She wipes her mouth clean and throws her napkin on her plate. "I'm done. I can't shove another bite into my belly."

"You ate it all."

"I guess I was hungry."

I grin. "Good, huh?"

"So good," she agrees. "Where to now?"

"How about a late outside movie at Cunningham Park?"

"I've never done that either," she says, clapping her hands in excitement. "Did you bring a blanket to lie on and everything?"

"I'm no amateur," I reply as I hand the waitress my card. "Of course, I did."

* * * *

"How long have they done this?" Fallon asks after we spread the quilt on the grass and I sit down. She lays her head in my lap, and I brush her dark hair off her cheek, enjoying her.

"I'm not sure," I reply honestly. "For quite a long time now. I don't usually come, but I thought it would be something fun to do with you."

She smiles and presses a kiss to my bare leg, just below the hem of my cargo shorts.

"It's definitely fun," she says. "What are we seeing?"

"An action movie. Last summer's Marvel blockbuster."

"Nice," she says, sitting up in excitement. "Anything with Chris Evans is a winner."

"Chris Evans?" I cock a brow and reach into my backpack for a bag of popcorn that I popped and brought along. "That's my competition?"

"There's no competition," she says, reaching in for a kernel. "He would win."

I pull the popcorn away, making her laugh. "I don't share my treats with women who insult me."

"Come on, don't be a sore loser," she says and brushes her fingers through my hair. "I mean, the odds of me actually *meeting* Chris Evans are slim, so I don't think you have anything to worry about."

"That doesn't make me feel any better," I inform her, but share the popcorn. The sun has set, but it's not completely dark yet. The park usually shows a family-friendly movie early, and most of the couples who brought their kids have packed up and gone home, leaving mostly adults in the park.

Fallon cuddles up to my side and lays her head on my arm, too short to reach my shoulder.

I lift my arm and wrap it around her shoulders, inviting her to scoot closer. She happily obliges me, and we spend a good portion of the movie snuggled up together until she gets tired and lies down once again with her head in my lap.

She's a sweetheart, there's no doubt about it. And I've grown used to having her nearby.

I've caught the glances from people I know, curious about us, and I'm sure sending text messages to mutual friends, asking what's going on.

I don't care.

Let them wonder. I'm not being coy. I'm touching her, and she's touching me back. I might as well be wearing a sign that says: *Yes, I'm with her.*

I don't like the thought of Fallon being fodder for the rumor mill, but there's no avoiding it when you live in a small town. It happens.

She shifts, turning onto her back with her head in my lap and gazing up at me, no longer watching the movie. She lifts her arm, burying her fingers in my hair above my neck, and pulling me down for a sweet kiss.

Yeah, there's going to be talk.

And I don't care.

Chapter Eight

~Fallon~

I don't know anyone here.

Actually, that's not true. I know Lauren, Jillian, and Cara. Oh, and Jeff and Nancy. I've now met Noah's parents, his cousins' kids, friends who are considered family, and it feels like I'm lost in a sea of people.

The King family is big, loud, and for someone like me who isn't used to big families, incredibly overwhelming. I'm on sensory overload.

The get-together today at the Lazy K Ranch is unlike anything I've ever seen before. There's a huge bouncy house for the kids, a group of people playing horseshoes on the opposite side of the main house, and still more kids running around.

I'll never remember all of the names, or who belongs to whom.

It's a lot.

But Noah is enjoying himself, playing horseshoes with Max, Josh, and Zack. Zack's son, Seth, is sitting on the wraparound porch with his girlfriend, a cute girl named Eloise. They're eating and laughing, looking at each other with soft smiles.

"Young love," Autumn says as she joins me. "I remember looking at boys like that when I was a wee girl."

Gray's fiancée is from Scotland, and her accent is hypnotic. From the moment I arrived today, she's been close by to chat or check in with me as if she knows this family is intimidating as hell and a lot to take in. Or, maybe she's as overwhelmed as I am, and we're in this together. Either way, I'm grateful.

"They're cute," I agree. "Seth definitely has the King good looks."

"Aye," she says with a smile. "They're hard to resist."

"When are you getting married?" I ask as we each take a cupcake from a table overflowing with food and walk to a table in the shade.

"Next summer," she says and grins. "But I've already been busy planning. I'm starting an event planning business here in town."

"Oh, that's wonderful," I reply. "You know, I was talking with Nina Wolfe last week. She's also starting a new business, and I think she could use your skills. Would you like me to introduce you?"

"That would be lovely," Autumn says, her eyes lighting up. "Thank you for the offer."

"Of course. I know how hard it is to be self-employed. I think you'll like Nina, she's great."

"That's right, Gray mentioned you teach yoga. Is that your own business, or do you work for a spa?"

"It's my own gig, and I contract with the Lodge on the lake for some classes, but mostly, I work out of a studio in the heart of downtown."

"I'll have to check it out," she says thoughtfully.

"I'd love to have you."

"Well, hello, you two." Noah's mom, Susan, joins us with her own cupcake. She's a pretty woman in her early sixties, with blond hair and a lovely smile. "Do you mind if I join you?"

"Of course, not," I reply, scooting over to give her room. "Are you having a good day?"

"Oh, it's always a joy to have the family together," she says, one of her signature smiles gracing her face. "I don't miss the winters in Montana, but I do miss being with the people I love the most. My boys tell me you're both new to town?"

"I've been here about two years," I reply.

"And I just found Cunningham Falls this past winter," Autumn adds. "Your son literally swept me off my feet. Or rather, I swept him off his."

She tells us about being up on the mountain and hitting Gray on the slopes. "I was so embarrassed, but it worked out in the end."

"I'm glad," Susan says with a laugh. "What about you, Fallon? How did you meet Noah?"

"I found an injured eagle and called for help," I reply. "Which reminds me, I should go check in on him. The eagle, not Noah."

"He's always had a soft spot for animals," Susan replies. "Even when he was young, he was always rescuing something. A rabbit, a bird. One time, he found an injured skunk and was so mad at me for not allowing it inside."

"Oh, no," I say, laughing. "I bet he smelled good after that."

"It was horrible," she agrees. "But, he has a kind heart."

"He does," I say with a nod and look over to where Noah's playing horseshoes. Gray has joined them, and they're all laughing at something. "I'd say you raised two incredible men, Susan."

"That might be the best compliment a mother can receive," she says, watching me closely before she turns to Autumn. "Now, let's talk wedding. I want to hear everything, and please know, dear, if you need me to, I can come up during the winter to help out. It would be a pleasure."

I listen for the next thirty minutes about cakes and flowers, dresses and parties. Autumn is intelligent and sweet, and I know her wedding is going to be absolutely beautiful.

"I'm being summoned," Susan says as she stands from the table and waves at her husband across the yard. "It's been so nice chatting with you both."

She hurries away, just as Cara and Jillian join us.

"Are you both overwhelmed?" Cara asks, a smile touching her eyes.

"A little," Autumn admits. "But in a good way."

"A lot," I reply with a laugh. "But everyone is super nice. It's just—"

"It's a lot to take in," Jillian says and nods. "Trust me, Cara and I have known the King family all our lives, and even *we* feel overwhelmed sometimes."

"Oh, good," I say with relief.

"We want to invite you both to go out later this week for a sip and paint," Cara says. "It'll be the four of us and Lo." She looks around. "I don't know where she went."

"I think she's feeding the baby," Jillian says.

"What's a sip and paint?" Autumn asks.

"We'll drink wine and paint pictures with the help of an instructor," Cara says and smiles. "I'm too old for dancing at the bar, you guys. I hate to admit it, but I am."

"You're not too old," Jillian says with a laugh. "You're too tired. But we still want a girls' night out."

"I think that sounds fun," I reply and nod. "I'm in."

"Me, too," Autumn says. "I'm all for trying new things these days."

"Perfect," Cara says. "I'll text you both with the time and address tomorrow."

Noah approaches just as Gray reaches Autumn. Noah pulls me to my feet and into his arms for a big hug.

"Are you about ready to get out of here?" he asks.

"Yeah," I say softly. "But only if you are. I can stay if you'd rather."

He smiles down at me. "I'm ready."

It takes us a half hour to say our goodbyes to everyone, but when we're finally in his SUV driving toward town, I let out a long sigh and lean my head against the window.

"Are you okay?" he asks.

"I'm totally okay," I reply honestly. "Just exhausted. People drain me. It's why I spend so much time alone. But I really liked everyone, and I had a great time."

"You can tell me if you hated it," he says, a smile tipping the corners of his lips.

"I didn't hate it at all," I reply with a chuckle. "Truly, it was fun. Seth was cute with his girlfriend."

"He'd better be using condoms," Noah says, surprising me.

"Do you think he's...?"

He looks at me and then back to the road. "Oh, yeah. He is. He's seventeen, and so is she, and they think they're in love. But if he brings a baby home, his dad will *not* be okay."

"Oh, I don't know," I say with another sigh. "I think Zack looks like the kind of guy who would be disappointed in his son and then swoop in and do whatever needed to be done to help."

Noah nods. "You're right. But let's not find out."

"Fair enough."

"Did my mom drill you?"

"No," I say, smiling at the thought of Noah's sweet mom. "She was so nice to both me and Autumn. Hasn't she met your brother's fiancée before?"

"She has, but only once because they met in the winter, and Mom and Dad spend most of the winter down south. So I'm sure she was happy to get to talk with both of you."

"I like your parents." I yawn. "How's my eagle?"

Noah looks at me, clearly surprised by the change in subject, but he smiles. "He's doing well."

"I'm going to have to check in on him soon."

"We can arrange that."

We pull into Noah's driveway. It's hot today, but not as hot as it has been, so I'm not necessarily in a hurry to go inside.

"Want to sit on the porch?" I ask.

"Sure, let's go around back." He takes my hand and leads me to the back deck. I sit in one of the deep, comfortable chairs and pull my knees up to my chest. "Would you like something cold to drink?"

"A water would be great."

Noah goes inside and returns less than a minute later with two bottles of water. He passes me one, then sits next to me and takes a long drink.

"The quiet is nice," he says softly.

"Mm," I agree, drinking my water, enjoying the way it soothes my dry throat. "You know, I've never thought about having a family. It's just never been on my radar."

He's quiet as I take another drink of my water, watching the tree line ahead. A doe and her fawn wander out of the trees and stop to watch us, their ears twitching.

"But maybe it wouldn't be so bad," I continue, thinking it over. "To have kids and a family."

Suddenly, my head whips over to stare at Noah in absolute horror.

"I don't mean today, or necessarily with you. I mean, I'm not saying I *wouldn't* with you, but I was just thinking out loud, I didn't mean—"

"Stop," he says with a chuckle and reaches over to take my hand in his, giving it a reassuring squeeze. "I didn't think you were proposing. I want you to talk about your thoughts. I enjoy listening to you."

"I don't know if I've ever felt this comfortable," I admit, feeling a frown on my lips. "I tell Claire some things, and Penny more than that, but I don't *confide* in either of them about much. This is new for me."

"We all need a person to confide in," he says softly. "And I'm honored that you're comfortable with me, Fallon. I'm not here to just have amazing, crazy sex with you. I want to be your friend, too. A relationship is both of those things."

"You're right," I reply with a slow nod, my mind still racing with thoughts. "I've always thought of children as a burden. As something to endure."

I frown and glance over at him, but he's just watching the deer and listening to me, still holding my hand.

"I mean, my parents? Not good parents. My mom was in and out like I told you before and couldn't be bothered with me. To be fair, she was about fifteen when she had me and was definitely not ready to be a parent.

"My grandma was wonderful. She was firm but loving, and I never questioned my place with her. But as an adult, I know that if she'd had a choice, she probably would have preferred her daughter not get pregnant in the first place. Like you were saying about Seth, having a child as a teenager is way less than ideal, and puts a lot of pressure on the family."

"Fal, I wasn't trying to imply that you—"

"Of course, you weren't," I interrupt. "I'm just still thinking out loud."

"Fair enough."

"But today, with your family, and Lo and Ty, and *everyone*…I don't know. I guess I saw a different side to what it can mean to be part of a family and to have children. They don't just love their kids, they *like* them. They listen to and enjoy them."

He glances at me now, his brown eyes full of concern.

"Did you not feel enjoyed when you were young?"

I pull on my lip, thinking it over. "It feels wrong to imply that Grandma didn't love me."

"That wasn't the question," Noah says.

"I think I was a handful for a woman who hadn't led an easy life," I confess, measuring my words carefully. "And I know that she loved me. But I *was* a burden for her. She never would have said that to me. Not ever. She was kind and incredibly important to me. But I don't really remember feeling like Grandma enjoyed raising me. She did it because she loved me and it was her obligation to do so."

"That makes me sad for you," he says, squeezing my hand again.

"Oh, there's no need to be sad for me," I reply. "That's why I didn't want to say anything. I *shouldn't* have. I didn't have a bad childhood in the least."

"Still, I wish it had been different for you."

"It was fine. I'm fine. But that's why I've never considered having kids of my own, or really settling down. But after today, watching the others, I don't know. I guess it seems kind of…*good.*"

"I think it could be good, yes," he says.

"But not today," I remind him. "Not now. I'm just saying."

"Right. Not today." He grins and takes a sip of water. "Have you ever considered reaching out to your mom? Maybe trying to have a relationship with her now?"

I shake my head. "No, I haven't. Let me see if I can explain this. You know when you have a relative as a kid, maybe an aunt or uncle, and you've met them a handful of times in your life? You have vague memories of them, but you don't know them. You've seen photos, but the person is a stranger to you?"

"Sure, I think we've all had those relatives."

"That's my mom for me," I reply, hoping he understands. "She's always been someone my grandma would talk about and show me photos of, and maybe once every five years or so, I'd see her briefly in person. But I didn't know her. I *don't* know her. And I don't feel the urge to seek her out. Not because of anger or resentment, but because she's not even on my radar. Does that make sense?"

"Absolutely." He stands and pulls me out of the chair, then lifts me in his arms and walks inside toward his bedroom. "Now, let's go back to the baby-making conversation. Just because you don't want one today doesn't mean we can't *practice* today. Just in case."

I laugh and lean in to kiss his cheek, rough from a five o'clock shadow. "That's true. You have some good ideas, you know."

He smiles proudly. "I really do. Here, let me show you my first idea."

* * * *

The sky through Noah's window is just starting to lighten up. It's way early, much earlier than I usually wake up. I would think that with the excitement of the family party yesterday, and all of Noah's fun, sexy ideas last night, I'd still be exhausted and out cold.

But I'm not.

I'm awake, and ready to start the day.

Noah, however, is still sleeping like a baby. His skin is warm and smooth, and I don't hesitate to drag my fingertip down his collarbone, back up his neck, around his cheek, and down his nose.

My God, he's handsome. With strong, masculine features, he could have modeled back in Roman times for their statues. I don't know what's in the water, but they sure make some pretty babies in

Cunningham Falls.

I can't believe I talked about having a family last night. I don't know what it is about this man, but my mouth just runs when I'm with him. I'm a person who could win an Olympic medal for keeping her mouth shut. I've been called a mystery. Cold, even.

But not with Noah.

No, apparently, I practically announce that I'm ready to start making babies with him. Which is just embarrassing.

But he laughed it off and showed me things I had no idea my body was capable of, God bless him.

His eyes flicker open, and he turns to me and smiles softly. "Good morning."

"Hi," I reply. "Can we go see my eagle now?"

His eyelashes flutter. "What time is it?"

"Five-thirty."

He frowns. "Why are you awake?"

"I don't know, I guess I just have a lot of energy."

He takes a deep breath and stretches his arms over his head, giving me a great show of flexing muscles.

The man has muscles for days.

He stands, his back to me and naked as you please, then pads into the bathroom. When he emerges, he reaches for his clothes.

"If you're going to stay in bed without any clothes on, I'll join you, and we won't go see the eagle."

I grin, not moving. "I'm watching you."

"A voyeur, are you?"

I bite my lip and nod. "I like the way you look, Mr. King."

He narrows his eyes and watches as I sit up and let the sheet fall to my waist, exposing my breasts.

"Fallon," he says quietly. "If you don't get your fine ass out of my bed right now, I'll pin you to it and fuck you into the mattress."

I spring from the bed and kiss him as I hurry past him on my way to the guest room.

"I'd like to request a rain check for the mattress thing," I call over my shoulder. I hurry into clean yoga pants and a tank, pull my hair up into a ponytail, then rush to the kitchen where I find Noah making himself a to-go mug full of coffee.

The kettle is boiling as well, and he's set out another tumbler for me.

"You're sweet," I murmur, hugging him from behind. I barely reach the bottom of his shoulder blades, he's so damn tall.

"Make your tea," he says, turning to plant his lips on the top of my head. "And let's go see your eagle."

"Okay." I grin as I get my tea ready, and then we're off, riding in his truck over to the sanctuary. We could walk, but he'll need his truck today, and I can walk back to the house for my Jeep when we're done. "Someone's here already?"

"That's probably Roni," he says with a smile. "She's an early bird, no pun intended."

"Has there ever been anything going on with you and Roni?" I ask, trying to sound casual.

"No," he says simply and climbs out of the truck. He opens the door for me, but before I can jump to the ground, he cages me in and leans toward me, lowering his lips to mine. The kiss is hot and deep, the kind you feel for the rest of the day. "You're my only focus, Fal. Jesus, I can't see anything *but* you."

"It was just a question," I reply breathlessly.

"And now I've answered it." His gaze, brown eyes hot with lust and something I can't quite label, falls to my lips. "You're so fucking beautiful."

"Back at you," I whisper. A car door slamming breaks the magic of the moment. "Someone's here."

"Yeah," he whispers, sounding almost disappointed by the interruption. "We'll finish this later."

"Finish what?"

"What you started in my bed this morning," he growls before planting another kiss on me and leading me toward the building. "You shouldn't feel insecure about any other women. They can't hold a candle to you, sweetheart."

"Well, okay then."

We take the sidewalk around the administration building to the one that houses some of the injured birds. Noah unlocks the door, and I walk past him, hurrying down the row of cages to see my eagle.

"Well, hello there," I croon, pressing my hands and face against the bars. He turns and looks me in the eyes, tipping his head to the side as I talk as if he's listening to me. "You're so gorgeous, sweet boy. Are you enjoying the royal treatment in here?"

"I was just going to feed him," Roni says from behind me, startling me. "Would you like to help?"

I glance over to Noah, but he just grins. "I mean, you're his human, after all."

"True." I look at the eagle again and smile. "Yes, I'd love to feed him."

"Okay, come on." Roni opens the cage, and we step inside. Noah closes it behind us. The enclosure is large, almost the size of a small bedroom. Roni carries a large syringe full of brown liquid and a plate with a pile of red meat.

"I'm going to start with some fluids and medicine," she says in a soft tone. "Good morning, fella. How are you doing today?"

She gingerly lifts him, careful not to hurt his injured wing, and tucks his talons in her gloved hand. She makes it look so easy, but I bet it's anything but.

"The fluids keep him hydrated, and the medicine will help him heal and not have infection," she continues as she urges the rubber end of the syringe into his beak and slowly presses the liquid into his mouth. "Good boy. Very good boy."

She hands the empty syringe to me, and I set it aside.

"There are forceps there," she says, gesturing to the silver pair on the plate. "You can take a chunk of meat with it and offer it to him. He won't hurt you."

"No, he won't hurt me," I agree and offer him some meat. He watches me for a moment and then eats the morsel of food eagerly. "You're a hungry little guy today."

I croon and feed, reaching out to pet the back of his head. He doesn't object to the affection.

"Oh, you're so soft," I say, offering more food. "And so smart. I wonder what you're thinking."

I finish feeding him, and Roni is patient as I continue talking to the eagle and petting him for a bit longer.

"Do you mind if I come to feed him more often?"

"Of course, not," she says with a smile. "If you'd like to stay with him, you can. I have to go feed the others."

"No, I have to work." I watch as she sets him down, and I crouch next to him, whispering to him. "You have a good day, and keep getting better, okay? I'll see you later. I'll come more often, I promise."

I follow Roni out of the cage and smile at Noah, who watches me with soft brown eyes.

"That was fun."

"You're a natural," he says, dragging his fingertips down my cheek.

"I have to go to work," I say and swallow hard. Whenever he looks at me like this, I want to strip naked and climb him like a freaking tree.

That wouldn't be appropriate here.

"Can I come?" he asks, surprising me.

"To my yoga class?"

He nods.

"Don't you have to work?"

"We have eight volunteers coming in at eight," he replies.

"I've got this handled," Roni calls from a few cages down. "I'll call if I need you."

"See?" he says and smiles. "I've been dismissed."

"Looks like you're going to learn some yoga today," I reply with a grin. "We'd better get going."

"I'm right behind you."

Chapter Nine

~Fallon~

He wants to learn yoga.

I'm honestly surprised. Noah doesn't strike me as the yoga type, not that there *is* a *type*, but most men think it's a woman thing.

In reality, yoga is wonderful for anyone and everyone, and I'm excited that Noah is curious enough to take a class.

But if I'm being brutally honest, it makes me nervous, too.

"You need a mat," I inform him and offer him one of mine. We just arrived at my studio in town. I don't have any classes at the lake today. "And you're welcome to set it out anywhere."

"I'll be in the middle," he says, looking around the empty room. He walks right out to the middle, unrolls the mat, and then walks back over to me and cradles my neck in his hand before kissing the hell out of me.

"What was that for?"

"I won't be able to do it for a while, so I'm getting it out of the way now."

He returns to his mat, leaving me with a crazy smile on my lips and every nerve ending in my body humming deliciously.

"Hey, Fallon," Brooke Henderson says as she walks into class. "Maisey's not going to make it today."

"Good morning. Thanks for letting me know."

Several others file in after Brooke, some with sleepy eyes, others bright and ready to go. Once they roll out their mats, they sit on the floor. Some stretch, others check their phones.

When it seems that everyone's here, I take out my own phone and ask if I can snap a photo for my business Instagram. Everyone agrees, and I quickly take the picture, then toss my phone into my bag and sit on my mat, facing the class.

"Good morning," I say.

"Good morning," they reply in unison.

Sam Waters hurries in and smiles in apology. "Sorry, Fallon."

"No worries," I reply with a smile of my own and wait while he settles in. "Okay, let's start with our breathing."

I take them through several breathing exercises, along with some meditation. It's my favorite way to start the day, and it helps me find my center. I can see stress falling away from my clients, their bodies both relaxing and looking stronger right in front of my eyes.

And then I spend an hour taking them through poses and flows. Some we hold extra-long, letting the worries of the day leave us as we focus on our bodies.

Noah is surprisingly flexible, but not unexpectedly strong as he moves from pose to pose. When he isn't quite flexible enough, I show him an alternative posture to get the same results.

When class is finished, I smile and say, "*Namaste.*"

"*Namaste,*" they repeat. It takes about ten minutes for everyone to gather their things, chat quickly with one another, and then file out of the room, leaving Noah and me alone.

"You're fucking incredible," he says when the door closes behind the last client.

"Why?"

He shakes his head as he climbs to his feet and walks over to the door, turning the deadbolt and locking us inside.

"Don't get me wrong," he continues as he turns and slowly walks toward me, his eyes pinned to mine. "I already knew that you were incredible, but watching you here, in your element? Fucking hot as hell."

I feel the smile spread over my lips. "Is that so?"

"Oh, yeah." He moves to stand less than two feet in front of me and reaches out to tuck a strand of hair behind my ear. "Your body is strong."

His eyes roam up and down the length of me, taking in every inch.

"Your voice is soothing," he continues, and suddenly boosts me up with my back pinned against the floor-to-ceiling mirror behind me. "And I want you. Right now."

I cock a brow. "This isn't terribly professional of me."

"No one's here." He kisses my chin and then my lips. Softly at first, and then deeper as if he's memorizing the shape of my mouth. His fingertips dig into my ass. Every muscle in his body is tight with pure lust.

"Noah," I whisper when his lips leave mine to make their way down my jawline to my neck. "Jesus, I always want you."

"Good." With me propped against the mirror, he leans back and rips my yoga pants down. One of the seams tears. "Why are you wearing panties?"

"I'm at work," I remind him, and he simply slips his finger under them and tugs them to the side. Just that contact has me writhing. "Ah, Jesus."

"You make me crazy," he mutters as he shoves his shorts down his hips, freeing his hard cock. He must have had a condom in his pocket because he slips it on and then plunges inside me, as far as he can possibly go, making us both gasp in pleasure. "Jesus Christ, you're snug."

"Feels so good," I pant, trying to circle my hips and make him move.

"The way you move your body is so damn beautiful." He growls before biting my neck, just this side of hard enough to leave a mark. The idea of Noah marking me is thrilling. He plants one hand on the mirror, grounding himself, and with the other wrapped around my waist, he fucks me silly, pounding hard as if he's a man possessed.

My heart thumps, and I'm panting hard, trying to stay relatively quiet in case there's anyone outside the door.

But man, he makes it hard to stay quiet.

"Go over, Fallon," he says. I reach between us and press my fingers to my clit and feel myself clamp down on him. "Fucking hell. You'd better come, sweetheart, because I'm about to lose it."

I couldn't stop the orgasm if I tried. And, really, who would want to try?

When we're both spent, gasping for breath and leaning against each other, Noah gingerly sets me on my feet, keeping his hands on my hips to make sure I don't fall on my face.

"Well, it wasn't a mattress, but I'll take it," I mumble and watch as he turns away to tuck himself in and do something mysterious with the condom.

I don't want to know.

"The mattress will happen later," he says confidently. "I'm sorry about your pants."

"No, you're not."

"No, I'm not," he says with a smile when he turns back to me and cups my cheek.

"It's a good thing I have a spare pair in my bag."

"I guess I should have asked before I tore them."

I laugh and kiss his palm. "It was a fun adventure. Thanks for coming to class."

"I enjoyed it," he says, and I can see from the look in his eyes that he enjoyed both the class *and* the after-class activities.

"Me, too." I take a deep breath and slowly let it out. "Now I have to get through three more classes today."

"I guess I should get back to work," he replies. "Do you need anything?"

I smile. This is Noah, always willing to help me in any way, anytime. It's something I've come to love about him, not because he does things for me, but because of his giving spirit.

He *is* a kind soul.

"I think I'm okay," I reply and lean in to place a kiss over his tender heart. "I hope you have a great day."

"If the way it started is anything to go by, it's going to be fucking fantastic."

He grins and lays a quick, hard kiss on me, then turns to leave.

I take a deep breath before pulling my spare yoga pants out of my bag. I guess I'll need to keep an extra pair handy, just in case.

I'm not complaining.

* * * *

"Is it a good idea to mix alcohol and painting?" Jillian wonders aloud as she takes another sip of her red wine and stares at the blue canvas in front of her. "I mean, I'm not good at this on a good day with *no* alcohol."

"If I couldn't drink wine," Cara says thoughtfully, "I wouldn't be here because I'd be too afraid to try."

"Exactly," the instructor, Jael, says with a smile. "A little wine helps to lower your inhibitions."

"I can't drink," Lo reminds us, laughing. "And yet, here I am. The things I do for you."

"Let's focus," Jael says with a laugh of her own. She's a pretty woman in her early forties, with red hair highlighted with blond. She's thin with kind, blue eyes. "Now that we have our base, we're going to add the silhouette of a mountain with trees."

"Oh, Lord, we're getting fancy," Autumn says. "I need more wine."

She hops up and fills her glass with more white.

I've barely had a chance to sip mine, I'm too focused on the painting. I don't want it to suck.

I'm just not super artistically inclined.

"Wow, look at Fallon's," Lo says, looking over my shoulder. "Have you done this before?"

"No," I reply with a shrug. "And I don't know if I'll do it again. I'm totally stressed out."

"No need to be stressed," Jael says with a wink. "Any mistakes can be covered up, and none of these are going to look exactly the same. That's the beauty of art."

"How long have you been doing this?" I ask, trying to follow her direction for painting a tree. "And why does this look like a penis?"

Cara chokes on her wine and then busts up laughing. "Oh, Lord. We have penis trees."

Jael patiently shows me how to fix my phallic trees.

"I've been teaching these classes for about five years," she says with a smile. "Since I got divorced, and my daughter went away to college. I wanted something to fill my evenings."

"You're an excellent artist," Jillian says, looking at the other paintings on the walls. "Do you paint for a living?"

"Aside from the sip and paint? No." She shakes her head. "I'm a nurse."

"Smart *and* artistic," I say with a wink. "You're a double threat."

"Not to mention, pretty as can be," Autumn agrees, making Jael blush.

"If giving you all wine inspires you to compliment me, I'll take it, but that's not the goal tonight. Now, we're going to paint in a full moon."

My phone pings in my pocket. I take it out and turn the sound off, expecting to see a text from Noah. Instead, it's a notification from Instagram.

Lacey McCarthy, my mother, started following my yoga page and went through to *like* every single one of my photos.

"Everything okay?" Autumn asks quietly.

"Yeah," I sigh. "Hey, let's take a selfie."

"Okay." Autumn leans her cheek against mine, and I snap the picture. It inspires a whole group shot, as well—all five of us.

"We'll take another photo of the group when your paintings are done," Jael says.

"I think that's code for stop goofing off and get to work," Jillian says. "Sorry. We don't get out often."

"You're a fun group," Jael replies.

I send the photos to Noah and tuck my phone back into my pocket and get to work.

An hour later, we're all sipping wine and looking at our handiwork.

"Not bad," I concede. "Thanks to Jael, mine isn't pornographic."

"Maybe you were just thinking about Noah's penis, and you transferred that onto the canvas?" Cara suggests.

"Ew," Lo says, wrinkling her nose. "If that's the case, Noah has a short, fat dick."

"He doesn't," I assure the room at large. My cheeks are warm from the wine. "I just got too excited about the tip. Of the tree. The top, I mean."

"Stop," Cara says, giggling hysterically. "Oh, man, I can't breathe."

"Zack and Josh have the same dick," Jillian says and sips her wine. "'Cause they're identical twins."

"Have you seen both of them?" Lo asks, mortified.

"No," Jillian says. "Cara and I just compared notes one time."

"I don't need to know what anyone's dick looks like," I say, shaking my head, grateful that Jael is in the back cleaning brushes and not privy to this conversation.

"Except Noah's," Autumn says with a wink.

"Well, yeah."

"Oh, Fallon, I meant to ask if you've heard from Penny?" Lo asks. "I know you're friends with her."

"I have," I say with a smile, careful not to spill the beans about the super sexy rock star she's currently banging. "She's doing great."

"I'm so happy to hear that," Lo replies, staring longingly at the wine.

"You can have a glass," Jillian says. "Just pump and throw the milk away later."

"It's too much work," Lo says, shaking her head. "I'm not wasting the milk. Some women make a ton, but not me."

I want to ask a million questions about being pregnant and giving birth and breastfeeding, but I keep quiet, just listening to the conversations around me. I know they'd answer my inquiries, but they'd also have questions of their own, and I don't have answers.

I'm not pregnant, and I'm not even getting married.

I'm just ridiculously curious these days.

My phone vibrates in my pocket.

Noah: *You're stunning. Sharing with Gray, he'll want to see.*

I smile and tuck my phone away.

"Noah is sending our picture to Gray," I inform Autumn, who gets a happy smile on her pretty face at the mention of Gray's name.

"Oh, how nice. Will you please send them to me?"

"Send them to all of us," Lo says with a smile. "And let's take more."

We're goofy, taking photos of ourselves and our paintings, of the wine, of each other, and for the first time since I moved to Cunningham Falls, I feel like not only do I belong in the *place,* but I also belong with the people.

I have friends *and* a man. A thriving business.

It feels damn good.

* * * *

"*Om shanti shanti.*"

My last class of the day is finally done. I'm ready to go home, take a shower, and relax.

"Hey, Fallon," Jenna says after she rolls up her mat and joins me. "I have good news."

"Awesome, what's up?"

"I have a cabin that just came available yesterday. I usually use it as a vacation rental, but I can totally let you stay long-term if you like it."

"That *is* good news," I reply with a smile.

"Would you like to go look at it now? It's literally down the street."

"Oh my gosh, yes. Let me just close up here." I tidy up the room and grab my purse and yoga bag, then lock up behind us. "If it's up the street, I can walk to work."

"That's what I was thinking," Jenna says. "It's a small house, but it's cute, *not* full of mold, and convenient to town."

The walk takes us less than ten minutes. It's a short distance from downtown, less than four blocks in a quiet neighborhood. Jenna wasn't kidding when she said it was small. The white house is tucked back from the street in some trees. The front porch is inviting.

"I know the yard maintenance is something you didn't want," Jenna says, pointing to the grassy front yard. "But I already have a service taking care of it."

She leads me inside, and I immediately like it.

"Oh, this is cute."

"I know," she says, grinning.

I wander through the small living room into a simple kitchen and then check out the two bedrooms and a bathroom. It's fully furnished, in newer pieces that are both trendy and comfortable. I like the style.

Not to mention, the energy of the space is calm. No ghosts here. The *feng shui* is perfect.

"You're right, it's small," I say as we step out back onto the patio. "But it's just me."

"Are you sure you want to move out of Noah's house?" Jenna asks.

I frown. "Of course. We're seeing each other, and I like him a lot, but we're not *living* together. Not like that."

Okay, so I've slept in his bed almost every night, and I guess we have been living together as a couple, but we always knew that would come to an end when I found a new place.

"Well, this is yours if you want it. You don't need to start paying rent until October."

"That's two months away."

She smiles. "Yes, and you've been amazing and patient with the whole situation. I appreciate it, and am happy to wait until October for rent. Please, it's the least I can do."

"Deal," I reply. Instead of shaking my hand, Jenna tugs me in for a hug.

"I'm so glad you like it." She pulls away and offers me the keys. "Here you go. You can move in anytime."

"Might as well be today," I say with a smile.

Jenna and I walk back to the studio where our vehicles are parked.

"Thanks again," I call out and wave before driving away toward Noah's place.

Honestly, I'm torn. It's a relief to have my own place again. Noah's house is comfortable, and I feel more than welcome there, but it's not *mine*. I've stayed there because he's kind and I needed somewhere to go.

Being close to the studio and back in town will be nice, although I haven't hated the commute from Noah's property.

I will have to drive out there to see my eagle, but that's okay.

I walk into Noah's farmhouse and take a deep breath. It smells like Noah here, and that's something I will miss. I'll miss being able to see him almost anytime I want.

But will that really change? I walk into the bedroom and start filling my bags with my few belongings.

It's not like Noah and I will stop seeing each other. We can still go on dates or spend the night at each other's houses. He's just a short drive away.

The relationship doesn't have to change.

I carry my things out to the Jeep, then go back in and walk through the house, making sure I don't forget anything.

The kettle Noah bought is sitting on the counter, next to the coffee pot. I didn't see a kettle of any kind at Jenna's.

I'm sure he won't mind if I borrow this one until I have a chance to go and buy one.

I quickly write him a note, leave it on the counter by the coffee maker, and head out, excited to get settled in my new digs.

Chapter Ten

~Noah~

"Fal?"

It's been a shit day. We lost an owl to lead poisoning, and one of the other owlets that Fallon and I saved that day on the highway is sick. We don't know why.

It's damn frustrating.

I've been looking forward to coming home and seeing Fallon all day. She's a balm to my soul and always lifts my mood.

But she's not here.

I wander into the kitchen to grab a bottle of water and see a note on the counter. Maybe she's going to be late?

Dear Noah,

Good news! Jenna has a rental for me. I checked it out this afternoon, and it's perfect. So I've moved in. The address is 689 Lookout Ave. Feel free to come by anytime! I hope you had a good day. I'll see you soon. Oh, and just let me know if I owe you any money for utilities or anything.

XO,

Fal

P.S. I borrowed the electric kettle.

I read the note twice, certain I'm hallucinating. She left?

She fucking left?

No phone call, no text. Just a quick and dirty note on the counter as if she's been my roommate for the past couple of weeks.

Maybe that's all it was for her.

I shake my head. Bullshit, it's more than that for both of us. She's just too fucking stubborn to admit it.

I crumple the note in my hand, grab my keys, and speed toward town in my truck. I'm not going to have this conversation over the phone. We're going to do this in person.

Fallon's Jeep is parked in the driveway, and Jenna's car is parked at the curb.

Good. Fallon can tell Jenna she's had a change of heart and won't need the house after all.

I walk in without knocking and find the pair of them in the bathroom.

"I promise, this leak was *not* here this morning," Jenna says with a sigh. "Damn it."

"It's a sign," I say, startling them both. Fallon turns to me with wide, green eyes. "That you're not supposed to be here."

"Hey, Noah," Jenna says with a smile and looks back and forth between Fallon and me. "So, I guess I'll leave you two alone. I cut off the water to the faucet so it should be okay." She stops, bites her lip, then waves. "Bye."

"Bye," Fallon whispers, watching me. "You're mad."

"Oh, fuck yeah, I'm mad."

"Noah, we both knew that I wasn't living there permanently."

"Did we?" I advance on her, wanting to crush her to me, but I wait. She stomps past me into her bedroom, pulling her things out of her bag.

"I never said I was staying with you forever," she adds, and it's like a blow to the heart.

"Are you saying this was just a convenient, fun time for you?" I ask, my voice deceptively calm. "Am I the schmuck here, Fal?"

"No."

"Because I've been over here, falling in love with you for weeks now, and you don't seem to have an issue with just jumping ship the second something else comes along."

"You...wait. What?"

"How does that surprise you?" I ask, dumbfounded. "I don't invite people to shack up with me at my house. I don't confide in them, let them submerge themselves in my life the way you have as if it's the most natural thing in the world. I introduced you to my family. This doesn't happen for me, Fallon. Not until I met you."

"Noah," she whispers, watching me carefully. She's gone pale, and the shirt she's holding falls to the floor. I hurry to her and scoop her up into my arms, relieved when she wraps herself around me, holding on tightly. "I thought I was in your way."

"Bullshit."

"I assumed."

"Don't do that," I reply and lay her on the bed, covering her with my body. Her head is cradled in my arms, and my pelvis is nestled between her legs. "You talk to me about everything else, and you didn't even consider that we should talk about this, too?"

"No," she admits. "No, because I'm independent, and I thought having my own space was the right thing."

I nudge her shorts down her legs and my pants over my hips, and when I'm free, I tip my forehead against hers.

"I don't have a motherfucking condom."

She smiles softly. "It's okay."

"Are you sure?"

She nods, and I don't argue. I slide home, buried to the hilt, and have to bite my lip to keep myself in check.

"Never done this before," I mutter.

"I disagree, we've done this plenty."

"Not like this," I reply and, still without moving, lay my lips next to her ear. "You're *mine*, Fallon. Do you understand?"

"Oh, yeah." She contracts around me. "I understand."

"I'm not going to last long like this." I ease out and back in, glorying in the feeling of her without the rubber separating us. "Damn it."

She wraps her legs and arms around me, holding on tightly. "It's okay. I've got you."

Her sweet words undo me, and I let go, crying out as the orgasm moves through me.

She's still holding me as I recover, brushing her fingers through my hair.

"You're *not* moving in here," I inform her. "Jesus, this place is falling apart."

"It's a leaky faucet," she says with a grin. "It's hardly falling apart."

I slip out of her, and once we're cleaned up, I start tossing her things back into her bag.

"Noah, I told Jenna that I'd be moving in here," she says, her hands on her hips. "I can't just leave on the first day."

Without a word, and with my eyes pinned to hers, I take my phone out of my pocket and dial Jenna's number. I put the cell on speaker.

"Hey, Noah."

"Hi, Jen. Hey, I'm just letting you know that Fallon doesn't need your place after all."

"Oh, I figured you'd just be there for the night," she says with a laugh. "It was pretty obvious you came to take her back to your house. I'm happy for you."

"Thanks. I can still pay you for the month if you like."

"Hey, this is *my* responsibility—" Fallon begins, but Jenna interrupts.

"Nope, we're good. Thanks, guys, and have a good night."

"Thanks."

I end the call and pull Fallon to me, kissing her silly. "You belong with me, sweetheart. Not across town, or even down the street. With *me*."

"Thank you," she whispers. "About what you said earlier."

I watch the nerves settle into her green eyes and try to soothe her by running my hand down her back.

"It's okay," I reply. "You don't have to say it back if you're not there yet. I know it's fast, but I can't help how I feel. And I won't apologize for it."

"I don't want you to apologize for it," she says. "I just...I just need some time."

"I've got all the time in the world."

I watch as she finishes putting a few things into her bag, and follow her to the kitchen where she retrieves her kettle.

"Are you ready to go home?" I ask.

"Oh, yeah. Let's go home."

* * * *

"So she's going to live there indefinitely," Max says two days later. We're having lunch at Ed's Diner, enjoying burgers and shakes and catching up on everything that's been happening. "I mean, I like her. She was sweet at the BBQ, and Willa enjoys her classes."

"But?"

"It's fast."

I cock a brow. "Dude. You asked Willa on a date and proposed like four minutes later."

"I've known her my whole life," he says but shakes his head. "You know what? You're right. Who am I to talk? I'm happy for you, and I *do* like her. She lights up when she looks at you."

"Yeah?"

"You haven't noticed?"

"I thought maybe it was wishful thinking."

He laughs. "No, I see it, too."

"How's Willa? And Alex?"

Alex is Willa's nine-year-old son. Max legally adopted him when he married Willa. There wasn't a dry eye in the place at the wedding.

"They're great," he says. "We're breaking ground on the new house this month. I'm hoping to move in next year."

"Gray mentioned that you hired him."

"Of course, I did," he says. "Gray's the best."

"Did the other lake house sell?"

"Not yet. I've been holding onto it because Alex likes the movie theater."

"We do have a movie theater in town, you know."

He laughs and shrugs. "Yeah, well, it's not the same." He checks his watch. "I have a conference call in a half hour."

"I have to go back to work, too," I reply and pay our tab, then follow him outside. "Since you still have the old place, we should have a pool night soon."

"Absolutely," he says with a nod. "And we can do a lake day with everyone. Boats and swimming. The works."

"Sounds fun. See you."

I climb into my truck and drive toward the house, my head already at work. I need to look in on the owlet that's been so sick. I don't know what's going on with it. We've tried everything. Part of me wonders if its failure to thrive is because it lost its mother.

I've seen it in bonded pairs. It just tears out your heart.

I drive down my lane, but rather than driving past the farmhouse to the sanctuary, I stop cold, surprised to see a strange woman sitting on my porch.

I park and hop out.

"Can I help you?"

"Oh, you must be Noah," she says with a smile. "I'm Lacey. I just came to see Fallon."

"Are you a friend of hers?"

"No," she says, uncertainty on her face. An uneasy feeling settles in my belly. "I'm her mom. I thought I'd surprise her."

I feel my eyebrows climb in shock. "This will definitely surprise her."

She swallows hard. "I know I should have called first, but she would have told me not to come, and well, I just thought it would be nice to see her."

"Well, she isn't here right now. But she should be here soon. Would you like something to drink?"

"Water would be nice."

"Why don't you have a seat on the porch, and I'll get you some."

It doesn't feel right inviting her into Fallon's home without Fal knowing that she's here. I don't know how she'll react to seeing her mother.

Something tells me she isn't going to be thrilled.

I hurry inside and grab a couple of bottles out of the fridge, and when I return to the porch, Lacey is sitting in a chair, nervously wringing her hands.

I see the resemblance now. Fallon is petite like her mom and has the same dark features. But Lacey's eyes are brown.

"Thanks," she says when I pass her the bottle. "So, are you her husband?"

How sad is it that a mother doesn't know if her daughter is married or not?

"I'm her boyfriend," I reply. I hear Fallon's Jeep driving up the road. "I think that's her."

"Great," Lacey says, but the nervousness is still there as she stands.

I watch as Fallon parks and hops out of the Jeep. When she approaches and looks up to see us, she scowls.

"Lacey?" she asks. "What are you doing here?"

"Surprise," Lacey says, tossing her hands into the air. "I saw on Instagram that you're in Montana now, and I thought I could use a vacation."

Fallon rolls her eyes, but then she narrows them at me. "Wait. Did *you* invite her here?"

"Hey, this has nothing to do with me." I hold up my hands in surrender. "In fact, I have a sick owl to see to, so I'll leave you to it."

I walk down the steps and offer Fallon the other bottle of water. I lean in and press my lips to her ear.

"If you need me, I'm right across the pasture. I can be back in twenty seconds."

She smiles up at me.

"I'll be okay. But thanks."

"I won't be long." I nod at Lacey. "Ma'am."

And with that, I leave, wondering what the conversation will be when I'm gone. I'm anxious to get back, just in case Fallon does need me.

Chapter Eleven

~Fallon~

I shouldn't have accused Noah of inviting Lacey here. He wouldn't betray my trust like that. I guess it was a knee-jerk reaction, seeing my mother after talking about her with Noah just a few days ago.

I don't like coincidences.

"Hello," I say and climb the porch, then sit next to her. She smiles, the lines around her tired eyes deep.

"Hi," she says and licks her lips. "I know this is a surprise."

"You could say that," I reply with a nod. "What brings you to Cunningham Falls?"

She frowns. "Well, you do, of course."

I tip my head to the side, truly confused. "Me?"

"It occurred to me the other day that I haven't seen you since your grandma's funeral," she says, smoothing her hands down her thighs. It suddenly makes sense. "So I looked you up on social media and found your yoga business. Fallon McCarthy isn't a super common name."

"No," I say while nodding slowly. "It's not common. Where have you been living?"

"San Diego," she replies. "For about a year or so, I guess. I met a nice man there. But, it was time to move on. You know how that is."

I know exactly how it is, and it suddenly hits me that I'm more like the woman who birthed me than I thought.

"What are you going to do while you're in town?" I ask, changing the subject.

"Well, I was hoping to spend all my time with you."

I sigh. "Lacey, I have a business to run. I can't really take time off to be with you all day. But there's a lot to do around here. I'm sure you'll find plenty to keep you busy. Where are you staying?"

She frowns. She expected to stay with me.

"I know of a vacation rental that just came open," I say before she asks if she can stay here. It may be heartless of me, but I don't want her to stay with me. "My friend owns it."

"Oh, that would work," Lacey says with a nod. "I'll get her number from you."

"Sure." I break the seal on the water Noah gave me and take a long drink. "How did you find me out here?"

"It's a small town, and like I said, you have an unusual name. I asked around and—"

"And it's not a secret where I am," I finish for her. "I haven't changed my phone number."

"I lost it," she admits. "I changed phones a couple years ago and lost all the contacts in it."

"Well, I'll give it to you again."

I feel so disconnected from her. She's a complete stranger to me. I'm not mad. I'm a little annoyed that she didn't call first, but I'm not angry. I don't feel *much* when it comes to her, and I wonder if that should make me sad.

"You know, if you don't want me here, I can just go."

She stands in a huff, and I stand with her but put my hand on her arm, stopping her.

"I'm surprised, that's all," I say, softening the tone of my voice. "And I had a long day. Why don't we make some dinner, and I'll call Jenna to see if she's rented out her rental?"

Lacey smiles, and it's like looking into a mirror twenty-years from now. "That would be nice. I can help cook."

"Okay." I lead her inside, and she smiles as she checks out Noah's house.

"You have a beautiful home," she begins, and part of me wonders if she's going to try to hit me up for money. She never has before, but I know she used to ask Grandma for money when she turned up.

I hope—desperately hope—that's not what this is.

"It's actually Noah's house," I reply as I set my stuff aside and lead her into the kitchen. "I moved in a couple weeks ago when the house I was renting flooded."

"What does Noah do for a living?" I glance over at her, and she holds up her hands in surrender. "I'm honestly just trying to make conversation, that's all."

"He owns the Spread Your Wings wild bird sanctuary," I reply. "He's a zoologist."

"Cool. I can't say I've ever met a zoologist before."

"Me either." I survey the fridge. "Looks like chicken Caesar salads for dinner."

"Perfect for summer," Lacey says with a smile. "I'll chop while you cook the chicken."

I'm shocked that the next half hour goes as smoothly as it does. We don't talk much, but it's not awkward, either.

Just when I'm about to pull the chicken off the grill, Noah walks in.

"We're having chicken Caesars for dinner," I inform him before he pulls me in for a hug. Damn, it feels good. I needed this.

"Sounds great," he says. "I'll go wash up."

"He's so handsome," Lacey says when Noah leaves the room. "You snagged a hottie, Fallon."

"He's more than a hottie," I say with a smile. "But, yes, he's easy on the eyes."

We set the table and sit to eat.

"How long are you in town for, Lacey?" Noah asks when he returns.

"Well, Fallon called her friend Jenna while we were cooking, and it sounds like the rental is available for three nights, so I'll be here until Friday."

"Nice," he says with a nod. "Summers are great in this area."

"I'm sure I'll find things to occupy my time," she agrees and looks over at me. "Maybe I can even talk my daughter into having lunch with me."

"I'm sure that can be arranged," I mumble and take my plate to the sink. Lacey and Noah help me clean up, but it's quick. Finally, Lacey loops her handbag over her shoulder and walks to the door.

"I told Jenna I'd meet her in about thirty minutes, so I'd better go." She watches me with sad eyes and finally reaches out to hug me. "I'll call you tomorrow."

"Okay."

I watch as she climbs into her car and drives away. When she's no longer in sight, I let out a long, slow breath.

"Jesus," I whisper.

"Are you okay?"

I look at Noah, who's standing behind me, his hands in his pockets. "Honestly? I don't know. I wasn't expecting that."

I tell him how she found me on social media, and feel my frustration grow.

"She may have *lost* my number, but she could have sent me a message on Instagram. Anything to give me a heads-up."

"Why do you think she's here?"

"She says she just wanted to see me. That's probably true. Like I told you, she usually grows a conscience about every five to six years and looks in on me. I guess this is that. She didn't ask me for money."

"Has she done that in the past?" he asks with a scowl.

"No, but she used to ask Grandma for it," I reply and sit on the couch. Noah sits next to me and pulls my feet up onto his lap. He slips off my shoes and rubs my arches. "You're good with your hands."

"Did she get money from your grandmother?"

"I don't really know," I admit. "I remember them arguing because Lacey would ask for it, but Grandma couldn't afford much. So, probably not. I think she was angry that Grandma left her things to me, but Lacey didn't even find out Grandma had died until a good week after it happened. We had to wait to have the funeral until we could find her. She wasn't daughter of the year.

"I inherited a small savings account, Grandma's apartment, and her personal belongings. And let me tell you, even when I sold the apartment, it wasn't a ton of money. But it was mine, and I know Grandma would want me to have it."

"Then what she wanted is what happened," Noah says. "Seems pretty simple to me."

"Me, too." I watch as he digs his thumb into my instep, and I sigh. "Should I feel guilty for not wanting her here? I know she wanted to stay here, and I immediately called Jenna. I know if it was your parents, you'd take them in in a heartbeat."

"My relationship with my parents is very different from yours," he reminds me. "She's basically a stranger to you, and if you can't say you trust her implicitly, then no, she shouldn't stay in your home."

"It's really your home."

He narrows his eyes on me. "Were you not part of the conversation the other night when we established that you live here, too?"

"I was," I say with a smile. "Point taken. And while I don't have a reason to *not* trust her, I don't know her well enough to say that I do."

"Then you did the right thing," he replies.

"She wanted to spend the next few days with me, and I told her no."

He raises a brow and looks me in the eyes. "You're not going to see her at all?"

"I probably should, huh?"

"Yeah." He smiles softly. "I know it's not easy, but you should at least go to lunch with her. Have a *real* conversation. You might learn something."

"You're smart," I say with a sigh. "I'll go to lunch."

"With Lacey."

"Yes, smartass, with Lacey."

"Good. Now, come here and kiss me."

"You're bossy." I crawl over to him and climb onto his lap, wrapping my arms around his neck and kissing him softly. "I kind of like it."

He plants his hands on my ass and squeezes. "I have more bossy demands for you."

"Yeah?" I smile in anticipation. "Like what?"

"We should go to the bedroom for the rest." He stands, carrying me with him and making me laugh. "The first one is to get these clothes off you."

"And the second?"

"You'll see."

* * * *

"You were right," Lacey says two days later as we sit in Ed's Diner for lunch. We're both munching on salads. "There is a *lot* to do here. Cunningham Falls is an adorable little town."

I glance up at her, holding my breath.

Do not say you're moving here.

"Oh, don't panic," she says with a laugh. "I'm leaving this afternoon."

"I thought you were staying until tomorrow."

"Well, while it's a pretty town, I think I've seen all there is to see," she replies and sips her iced tea. "I understand why you like it here."

"Where are you headed next?"

"Oregon." Her eyes light up in excitement. "I haven't been to Portland in about ten years, and I have friends there. It's such a fun city. Have you been?"

"No."

In fact, I thought that a little town on the Oregon coast might be my next stop before I decided to stay here in Cunningham Falls for the foreseeable future.

"Oh, you should go there," Lacey continues. "The city is just lovely, and the people are great, too. You'd like it."

"You know, I think I'm done moving."

She looks up in surprise. "Wow. Good for you."

"Why do you do it?" I ask, surprising myself but curious for the answer.

"What, move around?"

"Yeah."

She chews her bread and thinks about it. "I've always gotten itchy feet after I've been in a place for longer than a year. Maybe I get bored, I don't know."

I wait, wondering if she'll continue because I don't buy the boredom excuse.

"You know, I think I've been looking for what makes me happy."

"And you haven't found it yet?"

She shakes her head. "Apparently not. No city, no *man* has been able to keep me from wanting to move on. I guess I'm destined to be unhappy forever."

"Maybe you're looking too hard," I say. "I guess that's what I was doing, too. Traveling from place to place, trying to find something that felt real. Like I belonged there."

Lacey listens intently, her fork hovering in the air.

"I don't know if I've ever felt that way," she says softly.

"I get it. Maybe I'm more like you than I thought." I take a sip of water, thinking it over. "I loved Grandma so much, but I didn't belong in Chicago. So, I left. But I never stayed in any one place long enough to *be* happy there. I lived in St. Louis, Charleston, Austin, and Denver before moving up here, but I only stayed for a year or less before packing up and leaving.

"I don't know what happened here, exactly, except whenever I think of leaving, it makes me sad. I really love it here. And I've stayed long enough to plant some roots, make friends, make *connections*."

"You have Noah."

"Noah, and several friends. I've never been the kind of person to really connect with people on a deep level."

"I'm the same."

"And it's lonely," I continue, watching as tears form in her eyes. "I've found a place where I feel like I belong. I'm part of a community, and I feel important here."

"I'm so happy for you, Fallon." Lacey wipes a tear off her cheek. "I know I was a shitty mom. And I'm sorry for it."

"You weren't a mom, Lacey," I remind her. "I don't have any memories of you holding me or reading to me or teaching me."

"I know." She sniffs. She's not crying to be manipulative. I think for the first time in her forty-seven years, Lacey is doing some soul-searching. "I was so scared of you. You were tiny, and I was a baby myself. Thank God for my mother."

"Thank God for her," I agree with a nod.

"I know it's too late for me to be your mom."

"Yeah," I agree. I know I won't ever have the same connection to Lacey as Noah has with his mother. "But it's not too late to know me. We have time."

"I'd really like that," she says with a smile. "I'd love to be your friend. And when I leave today, it's not going to be six years before you see me again."

I smile, but I don't believe her. I've heard it before. As much as Lacey says she wants a relationship with me, I just don't think she's capable of it.

But you never know.

We finish our lunch, and I walk her to her rental car. She pulls me in for a hug, a *real* one this time.

"Take care, Fallon. I'll text you."

"Okay. You take care, too. Have fun in Portland."

She nods, already excited to get back on the road.

"Bye!"

And then she's off, and I'm standing on the sidewalk, watching her drive away.

I walk into the heart of downtown where my studio is located, but rather than go right back to work, I stop into Dress It Up, my favorite clothing store in town.

Okay, it's the *only* clothing store in town that isn't centered around souvenirs. Willa Hull owns it and carries beautiful clothes and shoes.

She's also one of the nicest people I know.

"Hey, Fallon," Willa says when she sees me walk through the door. "Thank God, you're saving me."

"From what?"

"Boredom. I don't know what's happened, but I haven't had a customer in over an hour. I can't change the displays any more today."

I grin and check out a green tank top. This one isn't meant for working out. It's soft and feminine, and I decide to buy it.

"Well, I was walking by on my way to the studio and thought I'd see if you have anything new."

"Always," she says with a smile. "Are you okay? You look like you have something on your mind. Let me make you some tea, and we can chat."

My first instinct is to decline, but I quickly remind myself that these are my people, and Willa is my friend. So I smile and say, "That would be great."

"I bought some of that tea you love at Drips & Sips," she says as she brews a cup of hot water in her Keurig.

"You didn't have to do that."

"Sure I did," she says. "You're a good customer, and you don't drink coffee."

"That was sweet of you, Willa. Thank you."

She sets the teabag in the mug to steep and then passes it to me.

"Now, tell me what's up."

"My mom just left town."

She blinks in surprise. "I didn't know she lived here."

"She doesn't." I give Willa a quick rundown on the relationship I have with my mother. "We just had lunch."

"I think it was brave of her to come," Willa says after thinking it over for a moment. "I mean, she knew that you'd be surprised, and maybe not excited to see her, but she came anyway because she wanted to look in on you."

"I hadn't thought of it like that."

"She may not have a lot of motherly instincts, but she wanted to make sure you're okay. And maybe for her, that's all she can do."

I nod and sip my tea. "You could be right. That seemed to be true the whole time I was growing up."

"You should shock the hell out of her and text her first and see what she says. If she doesn't reply, you'll know she wasn't serious about getting to know you better. But she could surprise you."

"That's a good idea." I pull my phone out of my pocket and send Lacey a message.

Me: *Hope you have a good flight! Safe travels.*

"We'll see what happens. Thank you."

"My pleasure. I'm a mom," she says simply. "I can't imagine not being with my child every day, but if that were my situation, I would want to reach out and make sure they were okay. It might be the only thing your mom knows how to do."

I nod again and set the tank top on the glass counter. "I'll take this for today."

"It's a gorgeous color," she says. "I just got these in."

I decide right on the spot. "I think I'll wear it on a date."

"Are you and Noah going out?" Willa asks with a smile.

"Yes, he just doesn't know it yet."

"Oh, I love the sound of that. I'll have to take Max out on a surprise date. He wouldn't know what to do."

"Look at us, being mysterious women," I say after I sign the credit card slip.

"Look at us, indeed."

"Okay, help the newbie out," I say, an idea forming in my head. "Where do the teenagers go to make out around here?"

A smile spreads over Willa's pretty face. "I like your style, Fallon. That would be Lookout Point."

"Of course, it is."

"And it's just up Whitetail Mountain Road…"

Chapter Twelve

~Fallon~

"You look so much better." I reach out and pet my eagle's head. I've grown brave enough to walk into the cage with him, and he lets me touch him. "Soon, Noah will be able to let you go, and you can get back to doing whatever it is that eagles do."

He looks at me and then turns his head again, blinking slowly as I pet his head.

"You like that, don't you, sweetie? Yeah, being petted is nice. I agree." I smile and enjoy the soft feathers under my fingers. "Noah's good at the petting thing. I was never really a touchy-feely kind of girl. I don't think that's my love language, whatever that's supposed to mean."

He turns and looks at me as if he's listening intently.

"But it is nice when someone you care about is gentle with you. Can you keep a secret? I bet you can. I'm going to take Noah on a surprise date tonight."

He tips his head.

"I'm not telling him where we're going."

He squawks, making me laugh, and I hear from behind me, "I think that means he approves."

I turn at Noah's voice and smile. "I'm glad I didn't give him any details. I had no idea you were snooping."

"Hey, I work here," he reminds me. "It's not snooping if I'm supposed to be here."

"I suppose you're right." I give the eagle one more pet and then step out of the cage with Noah. "Hi there."

"Hey yourself." He presses his lips to mine. "Whatcha doing?"

"I came to see my bird." I smile up at him. "And maybe you."

"I hear you have a secret."

I laugh and nod. "Yeah, I do. You need to be ready to go by seven."

"Tonight?"

"That's right."

His lips twitch, and his brown eyes are full of anticipation. "I have my orders. I'll be ready."

"Good boy." I slap his ass and walk away from him, his laughter filling the building behind me. "See you in a bit!"

The walk across the pasture is nice. It's still hot today, but there's a breeze, taking the edge off. There haven't been any forest fires so far this year, so the air is clean and light, full of the smell of wildflowers and pine.

It sure beats the hell out of smoggy Chicago.

I walk into the house and back to the bedroom to get ready. I'm officially moved into the master bedroom with Noah. No more guest room for me.

A cool shower feels nice. I even wash my hair, intending to knock Noah's socks right off when he sees me, making the half hour of blow-drying my long mane worth it.

I stare at myself in the mirror as my hair dries. I feel lighter than I did just a few weeks ago. I know myself well enough to know it's a combination of things. My physical training has been on point with all of my yoga classes and the little extra I do at the gym. And, mentally? Well, I'm home.

I haven't felt that way in a very long time.

I found my place, and I found my person. Happiness and contentment feels so much better than I ever dreamed.

When my hair is dry, I pull a wand through it, giving it a loose curl, and then I put on some makeup. Using a light hand, I use a soft foundation with sunscreen, neutral eye shadow that accents my green eyes, and a couple of coats of mascara.

It's amazing the difference a little makeup makes.

I'd just pulled on some shorts and the tank top I bought at Willa's today when I hear Noah come through the door.

"Sorry I'm late," he calls. "I'll hurry."

"You're fine," I say with a smile when he comes into the bedroom. He stops in his tracks, his eyes wide, and he slowly looks me up and down.

He swallows hard. "So, we're going to leave the house, and I have to control myself from getting you naked?"

"That's how a date works, yes," I say with a laugh. "You've seen me before."

"You're beautiful," he says, and I swear all my insides suddenly turn to a pile of goo. "I'll be in jail for beating all of the men up for looking at you."

"They can look," I say and saunter to him, boosting up on my toes to kiss him. "Only you can touch."

"Damn right," he growls and kisses me soundly, still not touching me. "I'm dirty. I need to wash up."

"Go ahead, I'm ready when you are."

＊ ＊ ＊ ＊

"This doesn't seem like the kind of food you'd usually eat," Noah says an hour later. We're at a bar downtown, the kind that serves the greasiest of foods and has a row of pool tables in a back room.

I grin and take a big bite of my burger. I only eat one a year, and this one is worth it.

"Sometimes, a girl has to let out her bad girl," I reply as I reach for my pool cue. "A little grease isn't going to kill me."

"You might kill me when you bend over in those shorts," Noah informs me.

"But what a way to go." I wink and circle the table, searching for my next shot. I'm horrible at pool. Maybe the worst in the universe. But I can look cute while I suck at it, enjoying this flirty game with Noah, turning us both on.

I lean over, making sure Noah has a view of my ass, and take my shot.

To my utter shock, I sink the ball.

"Not bad," he says, swallowing hard. He's barely touched his burger and fries.

"Aren't you hungry?" I ask as I reach for my fries and pop one into my mouth.

"Starving."

His eyes are hot as they roam down to my breasts and then move back to my face. This top has done its job, showing off my cleavage, but keeping enough to the imagination to make him want to see more.

Willa's got good taste in clothes.

I move to walk back to the table, but Noah snags my wrist and pulls me against him, burying his lips next to my ear.

"I'm going to do things to you tonight that you never even knew were possible."

My heart skips a beat, and I have to bite my lip to keep from gasping. After taking a steadying breath, I back up and smile. "Promise?"

"You are sassy tonight, sweetheart."

"I'm sassy every day, I've just turned it up a bit tonight."

"Any particular reason?"

I look at the table and take a shot. This time, I miss the pocket by a mile. "I'm happy." I shrug as I sit on my stool and take a sip of my beer. "And it feels good."

Noah brushes his thumb over the apple of my cheek before walking to the table and whooping my ass.

He sinks every damn ball he aims at, including the eight ball at the end.

"You've done this before," I say with a frown, sticking my lower lip out in a pout.

"A time or two," he says with a laugh. "Let's play again. I'll give you some pointers."

I perk up, excited at the thought of Noah pressed against my back as he shows me how to hit the ball.

"What just went through that pretty mind of yours?"

"I always enjoy having you pressed up against me," I say and step off my stool. "So, yes, please show me how to play."

"You're going to kill me," he mutters.

* * * *

"Where are we going now?" he asks two hours later. I insisted on driving tonight because I didn't want to tell him in advance what I had planned. I wanted it to be a surprise.

"Somewhere fun," I reply with a smile as I pull my hair up into a messy bun, trying to keep it from blowing in my face as I drive the topless Jeep. Once my hair is fairly secured, I start the engine and drive toward Whitetail Mountain, the opposite direction from home. "You'll like it."

"I won't argue with that." He sits back and enjoys the drive, and when I turn onto the mountain road, he looks at me in surprise. "We're going up the mountain?"

"Just a ways," I reply, not giving away our destination. Just about a mile before the ski resort, I turn down a dirt road and park at a lookout, where the entire valley is spread out before us. It's dark except for the lights from Cunningham Falls and the homes around Whitetail Lake. "Okay, you must know where we are."

He shakes his head as if he's confused, acting completely innocent.

"I have no idea what you're talking about. I've never been here in my life."

I laugh and reach into the backseat for the blanket I brought with me, then hop out of the Jeep and spread it over the hood. I gesture for him to join me, and we sit with our backs against the windshield.

"This is nice," I breathe, cuddled up next to Noah as we watch the lights below. The sky is clear, showing off the Milky Way above. "You don't see stars like this in Chicago."

"No?"

"No way. Too much light noise from the city and smog, most likely. This is just incredible."

"Look." He points to a shooting star. "Did you see it?"

"Yeah. There's another."

"I see." He tips his face down, watching me. "Thank you for tonight."

"It was just pool and Lookout Point."

A smile tickles his lips. "Best date I've been on in my life."

"Whatever." I giggle and straddle him, burying my fingers in his hair. "I think we can make it even better."

"I've wanted to get my hands on you all night."

"Nothing stopping you now." I shift my hips, grinding myself against the cock straining against his jeans. My shorts are little, and when he reaches between us and pushes two fingers under the hem, they slip easily inside me. "Oh, Jesus."

"I never got to third base up here before," he informs me. "It was so worth the wait."

My arms are wrapped around his neck now, holding on for dear life as I ride his fingers and kiss the life out of him. We're panting, and my heartbeat sounds even louder out here in the dark, looking out over the town I've grown to love.

With the man I love even more.

"God, that's good," I moan, just as a car pulls up behind the Jeep. We both freeze, staring into each other's eyes in horror. "Shit."

Red and blue lights flash. I hurry off Noah's lap then sit next to him, trying to look as natural as possible.

Of course, I'm right on the brink of a crazy orgasm, but the police officer doesn't need to know that.

A flashlight shines in my face, making me squint.

"Noah?"

I frown, trying to make out the person behind the glare.

"Brad?" Noah asks and then breaks out into laughter. "What the fuck is the chief of police doing checking out Lookout Point?"

"I got a call from a neighbor. They said they thought some kids were up here." He laughs and turns off the flashlight, leaning on my Jeep. "You must be Fallon."

"Guilty," I reply with a chuckle.

"Anyway, I thought I'd come up and check it out, shoo the horny teenagers along." He grins, enjoying himself.

"We were just enjoying the view," I say, shrugging innocently. "Nothing to see here, officer."

"Sure," he replies with a laugh. "That's why your hair's a mess."

I gasp and pull the clip out of my hair, letting it fall around my shoulders. Okay, so he caught us.

"Are we going to jail?" I ask.

"No," Brad says with a laugh. "Noah's dad would make me cut wood for the rest of my life if I took his son to jail."

"Dad enjoyed using chopping wood as a punishment," Noah says with a nod. "Not to mention, Max might be annoyed if you put his best friend in the slammer."

"My brother would just bail you out," Brad says with a grin. "We'll just save us all the trouble. But take the rest of this home, will you? It's damn embarrassing."

"I don't know," Noah says thoughtfully. "I got to third base with a girl at Lookout Point. I'd say it's something to brag about."

"Brag from home," Brad replies with a laugh. "Nice to meet you, Fallon. Have fun, you crazy kids."

"See you on Saturday?" Noah calls out.

"We'll be there." Brad waves, then gets in his SUV and drives away.

"What's happening Saturday?" I ask as I hop off the Jeep.

"Lake day at Max's place," Noah says and folds up the blanket. "I kept meaning to tell you about it, but you've had me so turned on, all the blood in my body is in my dick."

"I'm not sorry." I bite my lip and hop into the driver's seat. "Let's go home and finish what we started so we don't go to jail."

"I thought you'd never ask."

* * * *

I stumble into the bathroom and flip on the shower and adjust the temperature to steaming hot.

I'm running late, but I can't complain. Noah just showed me the art of wake-up sex.

Again.

I grin and step under the stream of water, careful not to get my hair wet. Since our date the other night, he hasn't been able to keep his hands off me, and I don't mind.

Not a bit.

I take a deep breath, enjoying the way the hot water falls over my sore muscles, and close my eyes, feeling the heat seep into my flesh.

It's been a busy, sexy week. A happy one, that's for sure. I only have one morning class today, and then Noah and I are headed to Max's lake house for a day of fun. I'd usually avoid such a big group of people, but I'm excited to see everyone today.

My eyes are still closed, but I can feel the shift in the air as Noah opens the glass door and steps into the shower with me. He drags his hand over my stomach before pressing himself along my back.

"Seriously?" I ask with a smile. "Again? We just did this twenty minutes ago."

His lips are in my hair. I feel them curl up in a grin. "It's not my fault."

"How is that?"

He reaches out to soap up my sponge and goes to work lathering up my back and ass. "You have these dimples, right at the base of your back. I love looking at them."

"Hmm." I plant my hands on the tile and lean forward, enjoying the attention to my skin.

"And this freckle, right here on your shoulder blade."

"I have a freckle?"

"Yeah, you can't see it." He kisses the spot in question. "But it's there, and I can't resist it. Not to mention when I kiss you right here."

He plants his lips on the back of my neck, just under my hairline, and kisses me before gently tugging the skin with his teeth, making me gasp.

"Yeah, that noise you make? Irresistible."

"Is that so?"

"It's the God's honest truth," he replies, and I turn to face him. Without thinking twice, I squat and take him firmly in my fist, jacking him slowly. "Ah, hell, then you do things like that."

"Do you like this?" I reach for the soap to wash our last romp in the sheets away.

"Who doesn't like this?"

I grin and watch his face as he leans on the wall, the exact same way I did. The water beats on his chest, sending a little spray over my head.

I guess my hair is getting wet, after all.

I don't mind.

When the soap is rinsed away, I lean in and lick his tip, around the lip of the head, and feel my core tighten when he moans.

He's not the only one that gets off on turning the other one on. It's a thrilling, powerful feeling to watch him come undone in my hands.

Because of my body.

I'm still moving my hand up and down in a steady rhythm as I feast on him, loving the musky scent, the visceral noises coming from him. When I slip one hand around his balls and suck hard, he cries out. The next thing I know, I'm on my feet and bent over, braced on the bench at the opposite side of the shower.

"You make me fucking crazy," he groans, slipping his fingers through my folds to make sure I'm ready for him.

It seems like I'm always ready for him.

"Everything you do turns me on, Fal. Every damn thing." He uses the head of his cock now, teasing me. "I can't stay away from you."

"You don't have to," I say, my voice breathless. "In fact, *don't* stay away from me."

He pushes inside of me, hitting a spot so deep in my womb it almost hurts.

"Are you okay?"

"Oh, yeah." I stand, shifting the angle a bit, and he leans down to kiss my neck. His hand is braced on my stomach, the other on my hip as he moves, pounding in and out of me until we're both spent.

"Convenient thing, shower sex," he says as he washes us both off. "You just leave the mess right here."

"So, that's what you're doing? Just thinking of the mess."

He grins, that sexy cockiness written all over his face. "Hell yes. I'm a giver."

I laugh and bite his shoulder. "I can't argue with that."

"Bite me like that, and we'll have to start this process all over again."

"I have to work." I slip from the shower and wrap a towel around myself, my skin humming from my second orgasm of the morning. "You keep yourself and your sexy ways away from me."

He turns off the water and reaches for his own towel, watching me with happy eyes.

"Fine. Only because I don't think I could survive round three."

"Oh, you could," I say with confidence. "We'll try another day."

He pulls me to him and kisses me deeply. Slowly. The tone changing from hot lust to sweet affection.

"It's a date, sweetheart."

Chapter Thirteen

~Noah~

"If you keep staring at her like that, people will think you're a stalker," Max says, mirroring my stance at the windows, our arms crossed over our chests. Fallon is down at the dock with the girls, sitting in the sun and laughing about something.

I can't hear her, but it makes me smile. Damn, I love her laugh.

"I don't know what you're talking about," I say. "I'm just watching the lake."

"Bullshit," Max says with a laugh. "You're looking at the girls. And it better be Fallon, because if you're ogling Willa, I'll punch you out."

"Same goes for Autumn," Gray says, joining us.

"I think we're all on board with that," Christian adds as he and Brad join us, as well. Here we are, a line of men watching our girls. Hannah is the first to jump into the water, splashing and swimming, urging the others to join her.

"That's my girl," Brad murmurs.

"She seems to be doing better," Max says, gesturing to Hannah. "She's much less anxious compared to last summer."

"She's working through it," Brad replies with a nod. "She never would have jumped into that water before."

"Good for her," I say, smiling as Fallon splashes Hannah with her foot.

"Looks like Fallon is fitting right in," Christian says, clapping me on the shoulder. "I like her."

"We all do," Gray agrees. "I'm going to be brutally honest."

"Oh, good," I say, my voice dry. "I was worried that you'd sugarcoat it."

"I didn't know if you'd fall in love," Gray continues, ignoring me. "Not because you aren't a good guy, but because you can be..."

"I can be what?"

"Abrasive," Brad finishes for him. "You're honest and blunt, and sometimes that comes off as douchey."

"I *am* douchey," I agree with a nod. "But not on purpose, and she gets me. We are honest with each other, and I'm learning to choose my words more carefully. The last thing in the world I ever want to do is hurt her, so I'm still me, but with prettier words."

"It's working," Max says. "She looks at you like you hung the moon."

"Which is how it should be," Brad adds.

"She's the best thing that's ever happened to me," I reply with a shrug, grinning when Fallon dives off the dock and surfaces with a big smile for her friends. "I never understood it before, you know? I watched you all fall, one by one, and I didn't get it. Until her."

"That's how it should be, too," Christian says. "Otherwise, we'd get married and divorced at every turn. You wait for the one that changes you. That changes everything."

"Listen to us," I say, laughing. "We sound so sappy."

"Love does that to you, too," Gray adds. "We're mushy. I can live with it."

"Me, too," I say with a nod. "Are we taking the boats out or what?"

"You guys go," Max says as he walks away. "I have to wait for the caterer. I ordered a taco bar to be set up, but they should be here anytime, and then I'll join you."

"I love days at Max's house," Brad says as we walk down to the lake. The girls have all climbed out of the water and onto the dock, where they're chatting.

"Who wants to go water skiing?" Gray asks.

"Can't we just go on the pontoon?" Jenna asks with a sigh. "I want to sit and watch the water and be lazy. I don't ever get to be lazy."

"That's one vote for lazy," Brad says. "Ladies?"

"I'm all for lazy," Willa agrees.

"Lazy," Hannah says with a sigh. "And safer."

Brad laughs and kisses his wife on the shoulder. "Autumn? Fallon?

Are you up for skiing?"

"I am," Autumn says, surprising us. "I'm trying new things."

"I can't let her go alone," Fallon says, looping her arm through Autumn's. "So, it looks like we'll go skiing. But I want to be lazy after."

"Deal," Gray says.

I pull Fallon to me and kiss her hard, in front of all the people that I love. "Don't worry, you'll be safe."

"I know," she says with a smile.

Christian and Brad join the other girls on the pontoon, while Gray and I take our women on the speedboat.

"Hey, wait for me," Max calls out and runs onto the boat before we can pull away.

"Did the food show up?"

"Yep, and they're setting up. Now, I get to play, too." He grins like a kid as we zoom out to the middle of the lake.

"Where's Alex?" I ask, wondering where the little boy is.

"With his best friend up in Glacier Park today," Max replies. "He'll be sad he missed this."

"There's plenty of summer left," Autumn says and smiles.

"You're right," Max says with a nod. "We need to do this more often."

"Where is the new house going?" I ask, scouring the shore but unable to make it out.

"Oh, good call. Let's drive past it," Gray says. "Take over, Max."

Max turns the wheel, taking us down the lake about a mile, then points. "Right there. See the crane?"

"Oh, that's going to be gorgeous," Fallon says. "What a view."

"It's not going to suck," Max agrees with a wink. "But we're about a year out from moving in. In the meantime, we'll keep the other house to use."

"Convenient, being a billionaire," Gray says, earning an eye roll from Max. "And, by convenient, I mean it works for me because I love lake day."

"He's using you for your money," Fallon informs Max with a laugh.

"I know," Max says with a shrug. "I should have caught on when we were kids, and he always borrowed money for extra candy at the movies."

"Whatever," Gray laughs and gets the skis ready to go. "Are you ready, angel?"

"I guess." Autumn doesn't look so sure.

"You'll be in a life preserver," I remind her. "If you fall, you'll still be safe."

"You've got this," Gray says and walks her through it. On her first try, she manages to get up and *stay* up for way longer than anyone I've ever seen on their first go.

"That was so fun," Autumn says when we pull her back into the boat. "I was a wee bit scared, but it was easier than I thought."

"You're a natural," Max says. "Because, trust me, it *is* hard."

"Your turn," I say to Fallon.

"No, I think it's your turn," she says, lounging in the front of the boat. "I said I'd go with Autumn, I didn't say I'd ski."

I narrow my eyes at her, walking toward her. "You're not going to try?"

"I don't think so."

I prop my hands on my hips and watch her smile up at me, squinting in the direct sunshine. It's hot today, but being on the lake is nice.

"I wouldn't mind watching *you* do it," Fallon adds.

"Ever the voyeur," I murmur and turn to march to the back of the boat. "Okay, I'm up. Let's do this."

I take off my shirt and toss it aside.

"Oh, yes," Fallon says. "Let's do this."

I turn to find her grinning, watching me. She likes what she sees.

* * * *

"I can't believe you went skiing without me," Alex says a few hours later as he munches on a taco. "Can we go back out?"

"Sorry, bud," Max says, ruffling his hair. "We're all skied out for the day. We'll go another time."

"Did you have fun with Pierce?" Willa asks.

"Yeah, but he got car sick, so we came home early."

"Going-to-the-Sun Road isn't for pansies," Gray says. "It's pretty, but it's windy."

"Yeah," Alex agrees. "What else did you do?"

"You're looking at it," Willa says with a laugh. "You're always afraid you're going to miss something."

"Well, I'm right. You went water skiing without me. Can we go get

Rocky from Grandma and Grandpa's?"

"In a bit." Willa gives him the you-better-change-your-tone mom look, and Alex sighs.

"You should have a dozen kids," Max says to Jenna, who just laughs.

"Hey, kids are good," Alex says.

"I know," Max replies. "That's what I'm saying."

Fallon slips her hand in mine and leans her head on my shoulder. It's been a full day on the lake with sunbathing, swimming, food, and even some ping-pong thrown in for good measure.

"Is anyone up for a movie?" Max asks.

"Yes!" Alex exclaims.

"Anyone else?" Willa says with a laugh.

"I think we're going to head out," I say as Fallon yawns.

"It's not the company," she insists. "I just haven't swum that much in years. I forgot how good it is for the body. I'll have to do it more."

"We're right behind you," Brad says.

"I'm surprised you didn't get called into the hospital," Jenna says to Hannah. "No babies being born?"

"I'm not on call today," Hannah replies with a grin. "And it was blissful. Thanks for having us."

"Anytime," Max says. "And I mean that. Willa and I are in town for a couple of months. Let's take advantage of the good weather."

"I'm down," Gray says.

"Unfortunately, I leave in two weeks to start a new film," Christian replies with a sigh.

"Being a movie star is important," Hannah says and smiles. "And I'm a big fan, so please make more movies so I can watch them."

"I'll do what I can," Christian replies.

"Are you going with him, Jenna?" Fallon asks.

"I'll go see him here and there," Jenna replies. "But, no, I'll be home for most of it."

Fallon and I stand, and the crowd moves with us to the front door. We say our goodbyes and hop into Fallon's Jeep, headed toward home.

"That was fun," Fallon says with a smile, pushing her hair off her cheek. "It was nice of Max and Willa to invite everyone."

"Max hosts a lot of parties similar to this one," I inform her, reaching over to take her hand and kiss her knuckles. "He caters, we play. It's a good time."

"There's something comforting about being with people in a carefree situation like that. No one working, no one cooking. We were all just there to relax, even Max and Willa, who hosted. I think it's a fantastic way to unwind. It's good for the soul. I feel very centered, and that doesn't usually happen when I'm with a large group of people."

"It makes me happy that you like them."

Fallon smiles as she turns down the road toward home. "I do. And you know what else I like?"

"Me?"

"Besides that."

"Tea. Green. Pistachio ice cream."

She laughs. "You remembered the whole list."

"Oh, there's more. You like it when I'm on top, and when I put my fingers—"

"Okay, okay," she says, laughing loudly. "I get it. You know what I like."

"What else do you like?" I smile at her, enjoying the hell out of her.

"I don't even remember now," she says, wiping the tears of laughter from under her eyes. She stops the Jeep in front of the house, cuts the engine, and sighs, catching her breath. Her eyes travel over the small farmhouse and the mountains behind it. "Oh, yes. I remember. Going home. I like going home."

I lean over the center console, cup her neck and jaw in my hands, and kiss her. Softly but thoroughly, the way I haven't been able to all day because we were always surrounded by too many people.

When I come up for air, she whispers, "What was that for?"

"I just love you," I say simply. I kiss her nose and then climb out of the Jeep, not expecting to hear the words said back to me. She's not ready. And that's okay because I see the way she feels about me in her eyes every time she looks at me. Each time she touches me.

Hell, just the words *I like going home* is enough for me.

She loves me.

* * * *

"Jesus," Roni whispers, surveying the scene before us. "What the fuck? Who would do this?"

I don't have an answer because only a monster could do this.

"There are at least a dozen eagles here," she says, her voice growing harder and angrier by the second. "Did you hear me?"

"I heard." I'm squatting next to a bald eagle, surveying the carnage. We're near a river, most likely where the eagles were hunting for food. "They've all been shot. Looks like with a rifle."

"They shot them for sport?"

"Poachers," I say with a grim nod. "Motherfuckers."

"Why?" She stares at me in confusion. "Why would anyone want to kill these amazing birds? They can't eat them. Not to mention, they're freaking protected."

"If we find out who it is, we can have them prosecuted," I say and walk to the next bird. "And the answer is, they did it because they can."

"Assholes."

"Agreed. Let's load them up."

"We're taking them?" She looks surprised for good reason. I don't usually move dead birds, leaving them to complete the natural cycle of life, but not this time.

"There's so many," I say grimly. "We might as well study them."

We load the truck, and just when I'm walking toward the driver's side, I hear a noise.

"Did you hear that?" Roni asks.

"Yeah." I'm looking up into the trees above the truck. "Fuck, there are babies up there, but I can't see where."

"There," Roni says, pointing to a nest about twenty feet in the air. "I saw a little head pop up."

"I don't have a ladder." I pull my phone out and see that I have a text from Fallon. I ignore it and call the office.

"Yo," Justin says.

"Not the best way to answer the phone, dude."

"I knew it was you. We have caller ID. What's up?"

"I need you to bring a ladder out here." I give him the details and hang up, then glance over to see Roni staring forlornly at the pile of eagles in the back of the truck. "Justin's on his way. He's bringing a carrier for the babies, too."

"Okay," she says. "You know, most days it doesn't get to me. I can handle seeing hurt birds. I mean, we do it every day. But when it's something like this. Something so horrible and *evil*, I struggle with it."

"I know." I swallow and stare down at the river. "I do, too. It means you're a compassionate woman, and you're good at your job."

"I wish my boss allowed day-drinking," she says, and I turn to find her smiling. "I could use a beer."

"Me, too. We'll have one after we get this sorted out."

We don't have to wait long for Justin to come driving up in another truck, the long ladder in the bed. He hops out and scowls at the birds in the back of my vehicle.

"What the fuck?"

"We asked the same question," Roni says, shaking her head. "There are babies in the tree."

"I'd like to have five minutes alone in a room with whoever did this."

"Same," I reply as I help him lean the ladder against the trunk. "You hold, I'll climb."

"Good, I hate heights," Justin says, holding the ladder steady as I ascend and find three little beaks greeting me. I have a satchel slung over my shoulder, and one by one, I gingerly take each baby and set it in the bag.

The nest is huge and brilliantly made. Looking in them never gets old.

I climb down, and we transfer the little ones into a carrier, then head back to the sanctuary. On the way, I make a call to the sheriff's office, informing them of the poaching.

They promise to keep an eye on the area, but the odds of them finding the asshole who did this are slim.

"I'll get the little guys settled," Roni volunteers, already carrying them to the building where we house the young birds. She's talking to them in a soothing voice.

"Poor little things," Justin says. "Maybe we should put some cameras out there. It's a hunting ground for eagles, and poachers know it. They'll be back."

"Agreed," I say with a nod. "I'll clear it with fish and wildlife. Let's get them set up today before dark."

"On it."

Justin rushes off to gather the cameras, and I make more calls, alerting the authorities to what we found and letting them know about the cameras.

It's late when we get finished, but I'm satisfied that if a poacher returns, we'll catch them.

"Thanks for your help," I say to Justin as he walks to his truck.

"Let's hope we catch the asshole." he says with a wave and drives away.

I walk home, breathing in the clean air and trying to clear the anger in my head.

Fallon's in the kitchen when I arrive, her hair up, wearing a little tank and shorts. Her usual. I can't resist her. I walk up behind her and hug her to me, relieved to feel her warmth.

I need her.

"Hey," she says and turns with a smile, but her face falls when she sees me. "What's wrong?"

"Rough day at the office," I say and bury my face in her neck, pulling her close. "You feel good."

She wraps her arms around me, holding on tightly.

"How can I help?"

Just that one question has my world sitting right again. I sigh, kiss her cheek, and pull away.

"You just did. What's for dinner?"

"Spaghetti." She shrugs. "It's easy."

"Sounds good."

"Did you see my text?"

"Damn it," I mutter, reaching for my phone. "I didn't read it because I was in the middle of a massacre."

Fallon: *Hey, sexiest man alive. I have good news! Claire's coming to visit.*

"Jesus, Noah, you can talk to me."

"I know." I smile. "But it'll wait. Is it okay if I take a shower before dinner?"

"Yep, I haven't started the pasta yet. The sauce can simmer."

"Good." I reach for her hand, pulling her with me. "Because I need you."

Chapter Fourteen

~Fallon~

"Don't forget," I say as I sip my tea, watching the sun make its way over the mountains. "Claire is coming tomorrow on the plane."

"That's right," Noah says, his voice still rough from sleep. "Is there a special reason she's coming?"

"My birthday," I say.

"What?" He stares at me as if I just grew a second head. "How do I not know when your birthday is?"

"I guess we've never really talked about it." I shrug. "When's your birthday?"

"Oh, no, it's not this week. Let's talk about you. When is *your* birthday?"

"Friday."

"Today is Wednesday," he says slowly and rubs his hand over his face. "When were you going to say something? Friday morning?"

"It honestly just wasn't on my mind," I reply with a laugh. "My birthday has never been a big deal. When is yours?"

"December fifteenth," he says, shaking his head. "I have three days to plan for your birthday."

"Seriously, it's no big deal," I stress. "Honest. Give me an orgasm, and I'll be happy."

"I'll give you a few of those," he says with a nod. "So, when does Claire arrive?"

"In the morning," I say, already excited to see her. "I'll pick her up, then take her to class with me. I only have one scheduled for tomorrow. Do you care if she takes the guest room?"

"This is your home, too," he reminds me. "I don't mind at all."

"You're pretty great. You know that, right?"

"Yeah, but don't let it get out." He winks at me, making me smile. "I'm glad your friend is coming. When was the last time you saw her?"

"Just before I left Chicago," I reply. "So, almost six years. We talk regularly, but it's not the same as seeing each other in person."

"That's a long time," he murmurs, watching me.

"Don't look at me like that," I say.

"Like what?"

"Like I'm a lost puppy. I have friends. I'm not lonely. Between Claire and Penny, I've had plenty of companionship, and let's be honest, since I moved here, I have more friends than I know what to do with."

"And I'm glad," he says, reaching out to drag his thumb over my cheek. "Because I know you're okay with keeping people at a distance, but you can't be an island, Fal. You need people, too."

"I have people," I assure him. "You're right here. The rest is a bonus."

"You're sweet," he says softly. "Do you want me to go to the airport with you?"

"No, you don't have to. I know you're busy, and you can meet her later in the day when we get home."

"Okay." He stands, ready to start his day.

"Have a good day, dear."

He grins and lays a sloppy kiss on me. "You, too."

* * * *

"You're here!" I grin as Claire pulls me in for a big hug, rocking us back and forth. "It's so good to see you."

"It's been forever," she agrees. "What are we doing today?"

"I have a class in thirty minutes," I reply as we walk toward the one and only baggage carousel in the airport. "So we'll do that, and then I'll show you around town a bit."

"Cool." She smiles. "I even went to a yoga class a couple times this week, just to practice."

"Good for you."

"That's me." She points to the leopard-print roller bag making its way to us, pulls it off the belt, and we walk out to the Jeep. "Will my stuff get stolen? Should we put the top on?"

"No," I say with a smile, fastening my seatbelt. "It should be just fine."

"I can't believe how small that airport is."

"I think they have plans to expand it," I say as I pay the parking attendant and pull onto the highway. "We're only ten minutes from town."

"The mountains are crazy," she says, looking around at the scenery. "The view from the plane was ridiculous."

I smile, excited and proud to show my oldest friend my home. It doesn't take long to get to downtown Cunningham Falls where my studio is.

"Where's the rest of the town?"

"This is pretty much it." I laugh as she looks up and down our tiny Main Street. "I *left* Chicago because I didn't enjoy the city, remember? It's safe here. Quiet. Fresh air."

"Lots of fresh air," she murmurs. "Is it safe to *not* breathe in smog?"

"You're silly."

I lead her up to the studio and pass a spare mat to her after she changes into a pair of yoga shorts.

Clients filter in, taking their places. Most of them say hi to Claire, who glances at me in surprise.

We're not used to strangers talking to us just for the heck of it. Watching her out of her element is entertaining, to say the least.

"Okay, everyone, are we ready?"

"I am if you are," Claire says. "Just go easy on me."

* * * *

"That was actually really relaxing after the flight out here," Claire admits as we drive to the house. She's calmer, with her face tilted up toward the sunshine. "I do love the weather."

"It's been a great summer," I agree with a nod.

"What's the population here?"

"Around seven thousand, I think."

She stares at me, surprised. "That's it?"

"That's it."

"Wow, you *are* in the sticks."

There's something about her attitude that's different from how I remember her. Her energy is different. I can't put my finger on what it is, but it's throwing me off.

"I like the sticks."

She shrugs, her blond hair blowing in the wind. It's too short to put up, barely brushing her shoulders.

"Do you ride horses and everything?"

"So, are you going to talk shit about where I live the whole time you're here? Because if so, tell me now so I can prepare myself."

"Oh, don't be so touchy. I'm just giving you a hard time."

"I love it here," I say firmly.

"I'm glad. Really." She pats my shoulder, and I can hear the sincerity in her voice. "It *is* beautiful. Just so different from what I'm used to."

"That's why I love it," I say with a sigh and pull into the driveway at the house. "Come on in. We'll get you settled, and Noah should be home soon."

"This is nice," she says as she yanks her bag out of the backseat and follows me inside. "Like, *really* nice. It's like something I'd see on that show with Chip and Joanna Gaines."

"Right? I agree." I quickly show her the main house, then lead her to the guest suite. "This is your space. There's a private bathroom through there."

"Great," she says with a smile. "Thank you for having me. It's so good to see you, friend."

"I agree." I pull her in for a hug. "Now, you get settled. Take your time. I'm going to make some iced tea."

"That sounds so good," she says with a sigh. "I'll be out in a few."

I shut the door behind me and walk to the kitchen, checking my phone as I go. I've missed a text from Penny.

Penny: *Hey! I know I'm a day early, but I wanted to be sure to wish you a Happy Birthday!*

I grin and type a reply.

Me: *Thank you! I miss you. Wish you were here for birthday margaritas.*

I set the phone aside and pull down the black teabags along with a pitcher. My phone pings behind me.

Penny: *Gah, that sounds so good! I miss you! What are your plans for your big day?*

Me: Claire's in town, and I think we'll just go to dinner with Noah. Nothing crazy. How are things with the hot rock star?

Penny: There's so much to tell you. It's good and confusing and wonderful. Sexy. So, so sexy.

Me: Bitch.

The three little dots appear as she replies.

Penny: You love me and you know it. I'll call soon and we'll catch up. Have the best birthday ever! Tell me all about it. XO

Penny's sweet. She was so fun to hang out with when she lived here. I was sad to see her go. But it sounds like she's living her best life in Seaside, and I wouldn't take that away from her for anything in the world.

I've just finished the tea and poured two glasses when Claire walks out of the bedroom wearing a fresh summer outfit. Her face is clean of makeup, and she looks much more comfortable.

"Better?" I ask, passing her a glass.

"So much better. I had to get the plane yuck off me." She takes a sip. "Mm, you always did make the best tea."

"Should we sit outside?"

"Sure."

She follows me out to the deck, and we sit in silence for a moment, drinking our tea and relaxing.

"I never thought I'd see the day," she says at last.

"What day is that?"

"You, playing house." She grins, but she's put me on edge again.

"I'm not playing anything."

"You're living with a guy, making tea, not thinking about moving on," she says with a sigh. "It's just *so* unlike you, Fallon. I'm concerned."

"You're concerned about my happiness?"

"That sounds horrible," she says with a frown. "I don't mean it like that. I do want you to be happy. I guess I'm just worried, that's all. Moving in with Noah happened so fast, and then you tell me you're living with him for good, not just until you find another place?"

"Did you come all this way to check in on me?" I ask.

"Sort of," she admits. "I wanted to see you, and I wanted to see this town, these people you've talked about. I'm looking out for you, Fallon. You don't have many people in your life who will do that for you."

"She has me."

We both turn in surprise at Noah's voice. He stands in the

doorway, looking as handsome as ever in a black T-shirt and dirty jeans from work.

"Hey," I say, standing to give him a kiss. "I didn't see you come home."

"You were having a pretty serious conversation," he says, his eyes softening when he looks down at me. "How was your day, sweetheart?"

"It's been good," I reply. "And it's better now because I get to introduce you to Claire."

"Hi," Claire says, standing to shake his hand. Her blue eyes check him out from head to toe and shine with appreciation when she smiles up at him. "Very nice to meet you."

"I've heard a lot about you," Noah says, a slight frown forming between his eyebrows. "I'll be right back."

He disappears inside, and Claire turns to me with a wide smile.

"I get it," she says. "He's fucking *hot*. I'd move in with him, too."

"Keep looking at him like that," I say casually as I pick up my glass, "and I'll throw you out on your ass."

She gasps in surprise. "I didn't—"

"Oh, you did," I say, cutting her off. "And it was funny when we were younger, but it's not funny anymore, Claire. It's not funny."

"I mean, he *is* hot."

I raise a brow, and she deflates, blowing out a breath. "Sorry. It won't happen again."

"Great."

What in the hell happened to my friend? Was she always this *bold*? This annoying? Is it that I've grown up, and she hasn't?

Or maybe I'm in love and territorial.

It's new, and I don't think I can control it. I'd feel the same way no matter who checked out my man.

I'm supposed to be able to trust Claire. I'm not saying I don't, but come on. Looking at your friend's man that way is in poor taste. I wouldn't do that to her.

"I'm back," Noah says, wearing clean clothes and carrying his own glass of tea. He sets his glass on the table, then scoops me into his arms and sits, settling me on his lap. He kisses my cheek. "You okay?"

"I'm great, thanks for asking."

"So, tell me about yourself, Claire," he says, reaching for his glass.

"Oh, no," Claire says, shaking her head. "You're the one with my best friend in your lap, so let's start with *you* telling *me* about yourself."

Noah smiles at her. Claire's not wrong. He's ridiculously handsome. And he's all mine.

"I was born and raised in this house," he says, gesturing at the building behind us.

"You're kidding."

"I'm not kidding," he replies. "I bought the place from my parents a few years ago and added the wild bird sanctuary at the same time."

He proudly points to Spread Your Wings.

"It's a great place," I add. "Noah rehabilitates injured birds of prey. Eagles, falcons, owls, osprey. You name it, he's got it."

"Wow," Claire says, looking at the buildings. "That sounds...interesting."

"It is," I reply. "Remember when you and I were on the phone when I went for that hike and I found the eagle?"

"Oh, yes, the eagle!" She nods with excitement. "Is he there?"

"He is," I confirm. "He had a broken wing, but he's going to be able to go free soon after he's healed up."

"That's awesome," Claire replies. "I'm glad you found him. I still don't know why you called *me*, but I'm glad he's okay."

"You called Claire first?" Noah asks.

"I didn't know *who* to call," I admit. "But I figured it out."

"Yes, you did." He pats my butt firmly, then turns to Claire. "What else would you like to know?"

"Do you have a brother?"

I roll my eyes, but Noah just laughs. "I do, and he's engaged to be married. Our parents are still married after almost forty years. They spend most of the year in Arizona but are here now for the summer. Let's see what else. I got 800s on my SATs, and earned a masters in zoology. I hate brussels sprouts. I'm not a serial killer, but I do own a firearm."

"I'll be sure to be on my best behavior then," Claire says with a laugh.

"Okay, your turn."

"Exactly the opposite of you," she replies with a shrug. "I struggled in school but did get a BA in accounting. My parents are divorced. I grew up in Chicago. While I'm not a serial killer either, I also own a gun."

"Really?" I ask in surprise.

"I live in Chicago," she says again. "You bet your ass I have a gun and know how to shoot it."

"Good for you," I say. "I've never shot a gun."

Noah frowns down at me. "We might have to teach you."

"I don't think I'm going to have to shoot anyone out here."

"Not a person," Noah says. "But we get animals that are dangerous, and you need to be prepared."

"So it's just as dangerous as Chicago, just in a different way," Claire says.

"Probably not *as* dangerous as Chicago," Noah replies. "But, yeah, we have bears, mountain lions, wolves."

"*Wolves?*" I screech.

"Yeah, they're a pain in the ass," Noah says. "A pack took out a whole bunch of Josh's cattle a few years back. They're not endangered like they used to be, so it's something we watch for."

"Jesus, remind me *not* to go for any walks around here," Claire mumbles, looking around nervously.

"You'll be okay," Noah replies with a wink. "Just carry bear spray."

"Wait. Do I spray it on myself?"

"No," Noah and I reply at the same time.

"Do that, and you'll land yourself in the emergency room," Noah says. "You just carry it, and if a bear or other animal attacks, you spray it at *them*."

"I'm happy right here," Claire says, shaking her head. "No need to get fancy and walk through the woods. I'll leave that for this one."

She points at me, and I laugh.

"Don't worry, we won't go into the woods while you're here."

"Good." She smiles at me. "Besides, we don't have time. There are birthday celebrations to be had, starting with you and me at the spa all day tomorrow. I've already booked it."

"Really? That's so awesome!" I clap my hands, excited to spend time getting buffed and polished. "I haven't had a spa day in way too long."

"You, my friend, are getting spoiled tomorrow." Claire holds out her glass to clink to mine. "And that's all there is to it."

"Well, I won't complain." I sip my tea, relieved that Claire seems to have calmed down. *This* is how I remember things being with her. Easy and fun, not full of snark and bitchiness.

It's going to be a fantastic birthday.

Chapter Fifteen

~Noah~

I'm nervous, and I don't *get* nervous. At least, not often. But I'm anxious about tonight.

"Are you ready to go to dinner?" Fallon asks, looping her arm through mine and smiling sweetly up at me. "I'm *hungry.*"

"I'm ready whenever you guys are."

"Claire should be out in a few," she says with a happy sigh. She's dressed in a beautiful red sundress, the hem hitting her at mid-thigh, showing off her gorgeous legs. I trail a finger down the thin strap on her shoulder, longing to push it off her and have my way with her.

But that'll come later. Or rather, *Fallon* will come later.

"Why did you just smirk?" she asks, narrowing her beautiful, green eyes.

I lean in and kiss her neck. "I was just thinking about all the ways I'm going to make you come later."

She takes a deep breath, her breasts rising and falling with the motion.

"I'm certain I've never seen anyone as beautiful as you are," I say. Her hair is pulled up with tendrils falling around her face. Her makeup is subtle, as always, but it's pretty.

"You look pretty damn good yourself," she says. "I like this shirt. Is it new?"

"Maybe."

I bought it today while she and Claire were at the spa.

"I think I'm ready," Claire says as she hurries out of the guest room. "I *know* I'm hungry."

"Me, too," Fallon agrees. "Noah, let's not take the Jeep. I worked too hard on my hair."

"The SUV it is, then." I hold the door open for the girls, and when we're all settled, I drive us toward town. "Did you two have a good time today?"

"It was *so good*," Fallon says, glancing back at Claire for confirmation. "Did you have Lucy for your massage?"

"Yes, and let me tell you, that girl has magic hands."

"She should put that magic in a bottle," Fallon agrees. "I'd buy it. I also had a facial and a mani-pedi. It was a full day of being pampered. Thanks again, Claire."

"I got to participate in all of those things, as well," she reminds us. "So, it was truly my pleasure."

"I'm glad you had fun." I take Fallon's hand in mine and kiss it, watching the road as we approach town. "You smell good."

"Thanks." She grins as I park in front of Ciao. "This is my favorite restaurant. It's Italian. You're going to love it."

"Spa and carbs, all in the same day?" Claire asks with a laugh. "Sign me up."

We get out of the vehicle and walk inside. My nerves are back on high-alert. What if she hates this? What if it pisses her off?

Maybe I fucked up.

"I have a reservation," I say to the hostess. "Noah King."

She checks her list and then nods and winks at me. "We have you upstairs. This way."

She grabs menus, normal as you please, and then leads us up the staircase to the room I reserved.

As soon as we reach the top of the stairs, the place erupts in chaos.

"SURPRISE!"

Fallon stops in her tracks, her green eyes wide as she looks around the room. My mom and Autumn decorated the space with green balloons and streamers, adding in other colors for fun. I had Brooke's Blooms outfit each table with a bouquet of summer flowers, and Maisey made the cake.

For only having a two-day lead time, I don't think it's half bad.

"Holy shit," Fallon mutters, staring up at me. "You did all of this?"

"I had help," I say with a wink.

"Happy birthday, sweet girl," Mom says, giving Fallon a hug. The room is full of the whole King family, including Seth and his girlfriend.

Not to mention, the Hull family. Between all of us, it's a packed room.

And, by the look on Fallon's face, she's overwhelmed.

"I—" She swallows hard. "I'll be right back."

She hurries away, and Claire moves to follow, but I stop her. "I'll go. Mom, this is Claire. Do you mind—?"

"We're great," Mom says, smiling at Claire. "Welcome, Claire. Let me introduce you…"

I hurry down the stairs where Fallon fled, and head for the women's bathroom.

I march right in without hesitation.

"You can't be in here," Fallon says, wiping at her cheeks.

"No one's ever going to keep me from getting to you. I don't give a shit what's on the door. What's wrong, sweetheart?"

"Nothing at all," she says, shaking her head and reaching for a paper towel. She dabs carefully under her eyes. "I must have something in my eye."

"Hey." I grip her shoulders and gently turn her to face me. "Talk to me."

She takes a deep breath and lets it out slowly. "I was *not* expecting that."

"That's the whole purpose of a *surprise party*. You're not supposed to know."

She laughs and lays her hand on my chest, just over my heart. "I know that, smartass, it was just so…*new*. I don't think anyone's ever thrown a party like this for me before."

"Well, then it's past time they did." I kiss her forehead softly, breathing her in. "Come on, they're excited to celebrate you."

"Thank you," she whispers, then launches herself into my arms, hugging me fiercely. "Thank you for the best birthday ever."

"You haven't even opened your present yet."

"Wait. I have *presents*?"

"Fal, I don't think you're grasping the whole concept of birthday parties."

She giggles and takes my hand, dragging me out of the restroom and up the stairs.

"Sorry, everyone," she says with a smile. "I had something in my eye."

"I hate it when that happens," Willa says, wrapping her arms around Fallon for a big hug. "You okay now?"

"Oh, yeah. Noah found it."

"I'm sure he did," Gray says with a laugh. Everyone takes their turns saying hello to the birthday girl, giving her hugs and wishing her well. Fallon introduces Claire, who is polite and friendly, as well.

I'm not so sure about Claire. I know that Fallon loves her, so I'll always be respectful and kind, but I'm on the fence about whether or not *I* like her. She can be brash in her demeanor, but then so can I, so I can't judge her too harshly for that. There's just something there, something I can't put my finger on, that rubs me the wrong way.

Ciao set up a buffet line along one wall. The cake is on its own table, surrounded by flowers. It's seriously beautiful. How Maisey pulled it together in one day is beyond my comprehension.

"I think she's happy," Dad says as he joins me at the edge of the crowd, watching everyone talk and laugh, wrangle babies, and go in for food.

"I'd say you're right." Fallon laughs with Cara and Claire. One of the girls put a tiara in her hair. "She was overwhelmed."

"We are an overwhelming family," Dad says with a laugh. "I mean, look at this. When it was just you four kids, your mom, Nancy and Jeff, and me, it was pretty tame. Now, we have little ones and friends, and it's loud. But I wouldn't have it any other way."

"Me either," I agree, my eyes pinned to my girl as she moves around the room. "I'm in love with her."

"Oh, we knew that. It's pretty obvious, son." Dad laughs and slaps my shoulder. "What are you going to do about it?"

"Marry her," I reply without hesitation. "Not immediately, but we're headed there. If she'll have me."

Fallon looks my way, and with a smile, sends me a little wave of her fingers.

"If the way she looks at you is any indication, she'll have you," Dad replies. "I'm happy for you. For both you and Gray. You found two wonderful women."

"I won't argue with that." I glance over to where Gray hugs Autumn, swaying to the loud music the restaurant plays. "Are you hungry?"

"Starved," Dad says with a smile. "It smells damn good."

"Let's go eat before Gray hogs it all."

* * * *

"Are you freaking kidding me?" Fallon says in excitement. She's opening her gifts, and just opened Willa and Max's present. "A shopping spree in your store? Willa, this is too much."

"No way," Willa says, shaking her head. "You're gorgeous, and an awesome walking billboard for my shop. It's really a selfish gift."

Willa winks at Fallon, who rushes to her for a hug. She gives Max a side-hug, and then Alex gives her a hug, as well.

"I have a present for you," Alex announces.

"You do?" Fallon squats next to him. "What is it?"

"You can come play with me and Rocky anytime you want," he says with earnest, brown eyes. "Rocky couldn't come to the party, but he's fun."

"I bet he's the *best*," Fallon says, giving Alex another hug. "Thank you so much. I'd love to come play with you guys."

"Cool," Alex says proudly. "And we can play video games."

Fallon laughs but nods in agreement. "Absolutely. You'll probably win because I'm not very good at it."

"I'll teach you." He shrugs and takes a bite of his pasta. "It's easy."

"Well, that's settled then," Fallon says with a laugh.

"I have something for you," I announce and pass her a little red gift bag with pink tissue paper sticking out of the top.

"This party is more than enough," she says with a frown but snatches up the bag. "But I won't pass it up."

I laugh as she pulls the tissue out. She frowns when she sees the black box at the bottom of the bag.

"What is it?" Claire asks.

Without answering, Fallon pulls out the long, black velvet box and clicks it open. Nestled inside is a diamond and emerald tennis bracelet.

"What did you do?" Fallon's eyes are glassy when they find mine. "Noah—"

"Do you like it?"

"What's not to like?" She laughs and holds it up to me. "Will you please help me?"

I fasten it around her tiny wrist, then kiss her knuckles. "Happy birthday, babe."

"Thank you." She loops her arms around my neck and offers me a sweet kiss. "I love it."

"You're welcome."

"Can we have cake now?" Zack asks, earning a glare from Nancy that makes us all laugh. "What? It's cake!"

"I say we eat cake," Fallon says, earning cheers of joy from everyone.

She cuts her cake, and I hang back, watching with a happy smile. She's having the time of her life, and I love that something so simple brings her so much joy. I'm also a little sad for the young girl who didn't have big parties to celebrate her birth.

Although I'm sure she would laugh and tell me to not think twice about it, I want to spend the rest of my life bringing this smile to her face. I want her to always feel special.

"This party was a hit," Claire says as she sits next to me, holding a piece of cake for me, and one for herself.

"I'm glad," I reply and take a bite of the white cake with strawberry filling. "How are you doing?"

"I'm having fun," she says with a smile. "I like seeing her happy."

"Me, too."

Maybe I've judged Claire too harshly. She's Fallon's friend, and she's looking out for her.

"What are you thinking?" She takes a bite of cake and watches me as she chews.

"About?"

"About Fallon." She rolls her eyes. "Like, what are your intentions?"

"Interesting turn of conversation," I mutter.

"Like I said yesterday, she doesn't have anyone else to look out for her, not like they should. So, I'm asking."

"I love her," I reply. "And I plan to make her happy for the rest of her life."

Claire looks over at Fallon, then sighs and pushes her half-eaten cake away.

"I was worried that this was the case." She wipes her mouth with her napkin. "Noah, Fallon won't be here forever. She doesn't stay *anywhere* for the long-term. It's just who she is."

I narrow my eyes at her, but let her speak. She's voicing every concern I've had when it comes to Fallon. I *know* she's moved around, but I also know the conversations we've had since we've been together.

Claire doesn't know shit.

"Fallon isn't the type to get married and have two-point-four kids with the dog and the picket fence." She shakes her head as if she's sorry to be the one to deliver the bad news. "She's *never* wanted kids, Noah. Not ever. She said she'd never let that happen. And settling down? Not likely."

"You've spent one day with her in six years, and you think you can say all of this with certainty?" I ask.

"We may not see each other often, but we talk all the time. She's my *best friend*. I know her, and I'm just telling you this so you don't get your heart broken."

I was right about Claire, after all. It sure sounds like she's trying to single-handedly sabotage my relationship with the woman I love.

"What are you talking about?"

Both of us turn at Fallon's voice. She scowls at Claire, her gaze bouncing back and forth between us.

"Claire's just filling me in on the facts about you," I inform her calmly. I want to scoop her up, but I'm curious to see how she'll handle this. "That you'll be moving on soon and wouldn't ever be interested in settling down."

Fallon narrows her eyes at her friend. "Is that so?"

"Hey, I'm just telling him what I know about you," Claire says with a shrug. "I don't want anyone to get hurt."

"Interesting," Fallon says, tapping her chin with her finger. "So you think you can just speak for me?"

"It's nothing you haven't said to me before."

"*Years* ago, and before I met Noah," Fallon says. "You don't speak for me, Claire. Not ever. And you…"

She turns to me, and I raise a brow.

"You and I need to step outside."

"My pleasure." I stand, and Fallon leads me down the stairs and out the front door. When we reach the sidewalk, Fallon rounds on me, her green eyes bright with anger.

"Did you buy that bullshit? Because that's what it is. Bullshit. I don't know what's up Claire's ass, but she doesn't have the right to say those things to you."

"She's not wrong," I remind her, tucking my hands into my pockets so I don't reach out for her. I *need* to hear what she has to say. "You do move on. And that's not conducive to a long-term relationship. She's your best friend. She should know you well enough to be able to—"

"Claire is *not* my best friend," she interrupts, pointing her finger toward Claire up in the restaurant and then down to me. "*You* are. You're my best friend, goddamn it. I told you, I don't let people get that close to me. Not until you. You're the one who knows me better than anyone else, and you're the one who should have told Claire to fuck off when she tried to ruin our relationship."

"I was about to," I reply and smile when Fallon stops short, blinking rapidly as she absorbs my words.

"What?"

"I was about to, and then you arrived. I know it's bullshit, Fal. Claire doesn't know dick about our relationship or how we feel about each other. She's been here for twenty-four hours."

"Well, exactly." She sniffs and smooths her hands down her dress. "Who does that? Who thinks it's okay to tell the man their friend loves that what they feel is wrong?"

"What did you say?"

She looks up with a confused frown. "What?"

I move to her and pull her against me, my eyes glued to her face, longing to hear the words again.

I feel like I've been waiting a lifetime.

Suddenly, her face softens in understanding.

"I love you, Noah King. I think I've loved you since you stood in my living room, ankle-deep in water with me. I'm just not good with words, and I—"

I crush my mouth to hers, swallowing the words. She buries her fingers in my hair and holds on tightly, pressing herself more firmly against me and turning me the hell on.

I want to carry her out of here and have my way with her, show her all the ways I love her.

But we have a birthday party to get back to.

"She was never going to ruin this," I say against Fallon's lips. "You can't ruin something so right with some careless words, Fallon. Let her talk. You and I know the truth."

"We do." She drags her hand down my cheek, her face soft with a loving smile. "I'm sorry she did that to you."

"I'm sorry she did that to *us*." I kiss her once more and then take her hand, leading her inside. "Now, let's go enjoy the rest of your party."

* * * *

"You look sad."

Fallon's just returned from taking Claire to the airport. It's early morning, the day after her birthday. The party wound down around ten, and when we got home, Claire went straight to her room and didn't come out until this morning when it was time to leave for the airport.

"I don't know what I am," Fallon admits as she puts on a pot of water to boil and gathers a mug and a teabag.

"Are you sad she's gone?"

"No," she says immediately. "I think I'm relieved that she left. I'm sad that things have changed so much."

She turns to me, leaning on the counter as she waits for her water.

"We met at the accounting firm I used to work for. She was actually on my staff, and we got along well. We became friends outside of work.

"After Grandma died and I moved on, we stayed in touch, stayed friends. That doesn't happen often when people move away."

"You're right," I reply, watching her.

"I guess this visit just hammered home how a friendship that's solely based on phone calls and text messages is so different from one in person. She's not the same girl I knew back then, and I guess neither am I.

"I *hated* that she ogled you that first day. It sounds stupid—"

"Not stupid."

"But I wanted to tear her eyes out. And it occurred to me, I wouldn't do that to her. If I was meeting someone important to her, I wouldn't check him out like that."

"I might have a problem with it if you did."

She smirks and turns to make her tea when the kettle starts to sing. She carries her mug to the table and sits across from me, cupping the ceramic between her hands.

"It was an odd visit. Sometimes, it would be like old times, easy and fun. Other moments were just uncomfortable. She enjoyed poking fun at Cunningham Falls, and she said she was *worried* about me, but that's not true at all."

"How do you know?"

"She apologized in the car," she says and sips her hot tea. "She said she was sorry, and that she was jealous of me, of what I've found here with you. I know she's been looking for a relationship. She'll take *anyone* home with her and tell me about it the next day."

"She's not going to find a relationship like that."

"That's what I told her. I don't think she heard me."

"Does this mean your friendship is over?"

Fallon shrugs one shoulder, her expression miserable. "I don't know. I told her I forgave her, but I'm still mad, and I don't know if I can forget it. I mean, how do you move on from that? Your good friend trying to drive a wedge into something really beautiful."

"I don't know."

"Me either." She sighs. "I guess we'll just see what happens. I know that it won't ever be the same as before. I feel like I've seen how Claire truly is, and I don't really like it. What did you think of her?"

I just grin and shrug, not wanting to say what I really think.

"You're the bluntest person I know, and you're not going to say anything?"

"I may be blunt, but I don't want to be an asshole."

"Did you think she was a bitch?"

"Oh, yeah."

She laughs and takes another sip of tea. "Well, she kind of was to you. I'm sorry about that."

"Not your fault." I tip my head, watching her. I hate the strain I see on her face. She may not let many people get close to her, but I can see it hurts her when the ones she lets in disappoint her. "What can I do?"

She stands and walks to me. I push my chair away from the table, giving her space, and she sits on my lap, laying her head on my shoulder.

"I could just use a hug."

"Always happy to oblige." I tighten my arms around her, holding her close. "I love you, baby."

"I love you."

Her phone dings in her pocket, and she pulls it out. She laughs when she reads the message.

"What is it?" I ask.

"Lacey," she says, shaking her head and chuckling. "She's wishing me a happy birthday."

"A day late."

She sets the phone on the table and wraps her arms around my neck again. "I guess the message is an improvement, even if she got the wrong day. She's trying."

"That's all you asked."

"Exactly." She sighs and kisses my cheek. "You always know how to make me feel better. Thank you for that."

"My pleasure, baby."

Chapter Sixteen

~Fallon~

"Hello?"

I clamp my phone between my ear and shoulder as I shove my things into my tote bag, ready to go meet Noah for lunch.

"Hey, Fallon, this is Rick Sheels."

"Hi, Rick, how's it going?" I prop my hand on my hip and stare at myself in the mirror, wondering why my landlord is calling. "I'm pretty sure I paid the rent this month."

"Oh, yeah, we're fine there," he says. He must be in his car because I can hear background noise. "I just wanted to give you a heads-up that I'm selling the building that houses the studio."

I frown. "The whole building? Even the ski shop below me?"

"That's right," he says. "I wanted to let you know in case it sells quickly, so you have a chance to find a different space if you want."

I sit on the floor, an idea forming in my head. "Rick, have you put the building on the market?"

"No, not yet."

"Would you mind giving me the first shot at buying it?" I swallow hard, butterflies setting up residence in my belly. "I don't know if I can get approved for the mortgage, but I'd like to try."

"Sure, Fallon. That would be great. Go ahead and think it over, talk to your mortgage broker, and let me know. I'll send you the appraisal so you can get things in motion. Good luck."

"Thank you. I'll keep you posted."

I hang up and tug on my lower lip, thinking it all over. I *want* this, more than I even realized. Glancing around the studio, so many ideas come to mind.

New mirrors, pillows, and mats. Cubbies for boots and shoes, a coat area. An infused water station.

There's *so much* I could do with the place if it was mine. So many upgrades that I'd love to see.

I check the time and realize I'm going to be late for my lunch date with Noah, so I grab my things, lock the door behind me, and hurry across the street to Little Deli. Noah's already sitting at the counter, talking to Mrs. Blakely, the longtime owner of the shop.

"There she is," Mrs. Blakely says with a kind smile. "Would you like your usual, dear?"

"Yes, please." I quickly kiss Noah, then climb onto my stool, letting my tote bag fall to the floor. "Noah, I need help."

"What's going on?"

I love the way he immediately snaps to attention, ready to slay any dragons in my way.

This time, though, *I'm* the dragon.

"I need a recommendation for a mortgage broker."

He frowns. "We talked about this two weeks ago when Claire was here. You're not going anywhere."

"Not to *move*," I say with a laugh. "Rick's selling the studio building, and I want to buy it."

He cocks an eyebrow. "Do you?"

"More than anything. There's so much I can do in there. I've been thinking about expanding my business for a while, but I didn't know how. This would open up so many doors for me."

"Would you let the ski shop stay?" he asks before taking a bite of his pickle. Mrs. Blakely sets my vegetarian wrap in front of me with a wink.

"Thank you." I turn to Noah. "I don't know, I haven't thought that far ahead. I probably would for now. My first priority is to update the studio itself. I have a ton of ideas for it."

"What's your end goal?" he asks, surprising me. "How big do you want to take this?"

"Honestly? I'd like to host retreats here. Incorporate good, healthy foods, yoga, meditation, and gratitude journaling. But I know that doesn't have much to do with the studio building and is something for later."

"We could add a few cabins to the property," he says, really digging in and thinking it over. It's like he's getting swept away with me, daydreaming. And I absolutely love it.

"You don't have to do that," I say, shaking my head. "Like I said, it's a dream for later. For today, I want to focus on this building."

"Would you still hold classes at the Lodge on the lake?" he asks. "I'm just trying to get a sense for your plan."

"Yes, I would. And I may work with Nina Wolfe in the future, as well. I guess I'd have to think about adding a couple of employees so I don't spread myself too thin."

"I think it's a great idea," he says with a nod.

"You do?"

"Of course. You're excellent at what you do, and expanding your business means you really are staying. For the long haul."

"For the long haul," I agree. "So, do you know someone?"

"I do. Evan Waters, Sam's brother. He's a mortgage broker. His office is just around the corner. We can walk over and see him."

"I *love* this small town," I say with excitement. "Everyone knowing each other pays off. Although, I shouldn't get too excited. I might not qualify."

"But you might, and you should at least find out."

"You're right." I finish my wrap. "You don't know if you don't try. I want to try."

"You're going to be great," Mrs. Blakely says. "It always makes me so happy to see new, exciting businesses come to town."

"You should come to a class," I reply. "I think you'd like it."

Mrs. Blakely smiles softly. "Oh, I'm an old woman."

"You're wonderful, and you might be surprised."

She wipes the counter down with her wet towel and then nods. "That sounds like fun. I'll come to a class."

"Wonderful." I reach down into my bag for one of my fliers that has the class times on it and pass it to her. "Choose any of the times on there. On me."

"Oh, no, I'll pay you."

"Not for your first class," I insist. "If you enjoy it and you want to keep coming, we'll take it from there."

"You have yourself a deal, young lady."

"See? You're a natural businesswoman. Let's go get you that loan."

Noah pays for our lunch, takes my hand, and escorts me out of the deli and down the block. We turn right at the end of the street and, sure enough, Evan Waters' office is right there.

"Hi, Noah," the receptionist says with a smile. "How can I help you?"

"Is Evan in? We don't have an appointment."

"I sure am," Evan calls from his office. "Come on back."

"Hey, man," Noah says, offering his hand for Evan to shake. "We're here for my girlfriend, Fallon McCarthy."

"That would be me," I say with a smile and shake Evan's hand. "If I didn't know better, I'd say you're Sam's twin."

"He's a year younger than me," Evan says, laughing. "And I'm the better-looking one. So, tell me what's up."

"Rick Sheels owns the building that houses my yoga business. I just received a call from him today that he's going to sell it, and I'd like to buy it."

"Really?" Evan's eyebrows climb in surprise. "Do you have an appraisal?"

"He was going to email it to me." I open my inbox on my phone and smile. "Yep, here it is."

I check it out and feel my eyes just about bug out of my head at the price.

"Holy shit."

"How much?" Evan asks. I tell him, and he whistles. "Well, it's in downtown, and real estate is at a premium down here. It's not cheap. Do you think you can afford this?"

"It depends on what the mortgage would be."

He crunches some numbers on the computer and turns it to me. The figure is a bit intimidating, but not outside the realm of possibility, especially in the busier months.

"I can do this," I say with confidence. "What do you need from me?"

"A lot," he says with a laugh. "Let's start with…"

* * * *

"Are you freaking kidding me?" I ask two weeks later, stunned as Evan just smiles from across his desk. "I'm *approved*?"

"That's not all," he says. "I was able to get the loan for fifty thousand more than the asking price, so you can do the upgrades you want. It didn't move your mortgage amount by much, and it gives you a lot of wiggle room. The business plan you wrote up was incredible, Fallon. You did a great job."

"Holy shit," I whisper, my hands covering my mouth. "It's mine."

"Well, in forty days it will officially be yours," he says. "That gives you time to get everything ready to go."

"But I don't have to move out. I can continue my classes."

"Absolutely."

"If I wasn't madly in love with Noah, I would kiss you on the mouth right now."

Evan laughs as he stands from his desk and shakes my hand.

"Congratulations. I'll call you when we're ready to close, and I have all of the paperwork for you. That's when you sign your life away."

"I can't wait." I do a little happy dance as I leave the office and call Noah.

"Give me the good news, sweetheart."

"I got it!" I'm practically skipping down the street toward my Jeep, still parked in front of the studio. "They approved me."

"Of course, they did. I never doubted you. All of those sleepless nights and worry was for nothing."

"Not for nothing," I say as I approach the studio and see Noah standing outside, his phone pressed to his ear. "This is my dream we're talking about."

"You're right," he says, his brown eyes shining as I approach. We're both still talking into our phones. "It's incredibly important, and I'm so proud of you, Fal."

"Thanks. We should hang up now."

He clicks off and shoves his phone into his pocket as I lead him up the stairs to the studio.

"Okay, tell me what you see."

"First, I need pretty cubbies along this wall"—I point at the space just inside the door—"for my clients to store their belongings during class. I want to replace the wall of mirrors, and I want an infused water station over there."

"Infused water?"

"You know, with cucumber, strawberries, blueberries. It's delicious and so good for you. And then, over here—"

Before I can finish my sentence, Noah scoops me into his arms and kisses the hell out of me, making all coherent thought scatter like spilled sand.

When he comes up for a breath, I smile. "What was that for?"

"You're sexy when you have your bossy hat on."

"Well, that's good, because I plan to be bossy often when it comes to this business."

"Works for me."

He pins me against the mirror, and his hand dives under my tank and up to my breast, worrying the nipple between his thumb and forefinger.

"Jesus, I can't get enough of you," he growls.

"No complaints here," I reply and unfasten his jeans. But just when my hand folds around his cock, there's a knock on the door.

"Fallon?" Gray calls out.

"I hate my brother," Noah mutters, readjusting himself with a pained expression on his handsome face. "What's he doing here?"

"I asked him to come," I inform him. "I have remodeling questions. Are you okay?"

"No." He sighs. "Go ahead and open it."

Gray grins when I open the door, then laughs when he sees his brother. "Did I interrupt something?"

"Yes. Go away," Noah says, but I roll my eyes and step back.

"Come in," I reply. "This won't take long. I won't take possession of ownership for about six weeks, but I want to show you my ideas so you know what I want."

I go through everything I just showed Noah.

"Also, I need more shelves over here for new mats and pillows. I also want a new desk for over here."

"You're going to have him build you a desk?" Noah asks.

"No, I'm going to buy one, I'm just thinking out loud."

"I'll put in an order for the mirrors now," Gray says, making notes. "Those could take a while. Do you want to replace this floor? It's pretty beat-up."

"I don't want to spend a fortune," I say, biting my lip.

"I have an idea." Gray reaches for his phone and taps the screen, then turns it to me. "This is a laminate floor. It's durable, and you can't tell that it's not hardwood."

"It's gorgeous."

"It's also a quarter of the price of hardwood."

"Seriously?" I enlarge the photo, getting a closer look. "Okay, you've sold me. Let's do it."

"I'll put that on order, as well," he replies. "As long as all of the supplies arrive, this shouldn't take longer than a week to do."

I cock a brow. "Didn't you say that about my former living room? Is that place done yet?"

"Don't try to be funny, Fallon," Gray says with a scowl. "It doesn't work."

"I don't know what you're talking about. I'm freaking hilarious."

"Keep me posted on when you want me to start this. I'll have a crew handy for you."

"Thank you," I say seriously. "I know you're busy, and I appreciate you making time for me."

"That's what family does," he replies simply before he leaves.

"But I'm not—"

"Yeah," Noah says, rubbing my shoulders from behind. "You're family, whether you like it or not."

"I think I like it," I whisper before turning and wrapping my arms around Noah's middle. "I like it a lot."

Chapter Seventeen

~Fallon~

"Honey, I'm home," I call as I walk into the house later that night. I've started hosting an evening class twice a week for people who work during the day, and so far, they've been a big hit.

But it also puts me home later than usual. It's almost dark outside, and as we're nearing the end of summer, that means it's late.

I'm starving, and I'm ready to wind down for the night.

"In the kitchen," Noah calls back. "But don't come in here yet. Go change or something."

"What are you doing?" I ask with a smile.

"None of your business." His voice is full of laughter. "Seriously, give me ten minutes here."

"Okay, I'll go change."

I wander into our bedroom and drop my bag on the floor before peeling out of the yoga pants and tank I've been wearing all day. I reach for a pair of shorts and a T-shirt that says *Namaste in bed*, tug them both on and check my phone.

I haven't heard from Claire since she left here a few weeks ago. I also haven't contacted her. Part of me feels a little guilty, but I'm still so angry, and I guess she's not the friend I thought she was.

I don't know if we'll mend our friendship.

I spoke with Penny a few days ago and filled her in on everything going on, including my purchase of the studio. She was so truly happy for me and excited, it reminded me that *that's* what true friendship looks like.

"Where are you?"

I open the bedroom door and smile as Noah walks toward me. He's in faded blue jeans and a yellow, button-down shirt.

"You look fancy. Am I underdressed?"

"No, I'm going to get you out of all of your clothes soon," he says, making me laugh. He kisses my hand, then leads me into the kitchen.

There are candles lit, flowers on the table, and grilled salmon plated with wild rice and green beans.

"Noah," I say with a sigh. "You did all this?"

"We have to celebrate," he replies as he pulls a chair out for me to sit in. "It's not every day my girl buys a building for her business."

"No, it's not," I say with a smile and breathe in the smell of the amazing plate of food in front of me. "This looks absolutely delicious."

"Yes, it does."

I glance up and find him looking at me with those deep brown eyes full of lust and appreciation.

"You're such a flirt."

"Only with you, sweetheart." He waits while I take a bite of dinner. "Well?"

"Maybe the best fish I've ever eaten."

He grins. "Now you're just being nice."

"No way." I shake my head and take another bite. "We're honest, remember?"

"That's not all I remember." He holds up a bottle of wine. "Would you like some pinot gris?"

"That sounds perfect."

He pours the wine into our glasses, then holds his up for a toast. "To you and your incredible passion for your business. You've done an amazing job making your dreams come true, and I couldn't be prouder of you, Fal."

"Thank you." I clink my glass to his. "And before we drink, I also have a toast. To *you*. For believing in me, and your unwavering support during this whole stressful, difficult process. I don't know if I would have survived it without you, and I appreciate you."

We clink once more and take sips of the wine.

"We're pretty good as a team," he says as he eats his dinner. "And the offer to build some cabins out here for your retreats is still open."

"I'm not comfortable with that," I admit. "Noah, this is *your* property. And, yes, I live here with you, and I love it, but it's yours."

He narrows his eyes but surprises me with, "I get it. I won't mention it again for now."

"You're agreeable."

"You make sense," he says. "Guess what?"

"What's that?"

"Your eagle is all healed up."

I stare at him in surprise. "Really? So soon?"

"It's been over six weeks," he replies with a smile. "Time just flies when you're having fun."

"Wow," I breathe. "When will you let him go?"

"We're going to take a couple of days to check his blood and get him a little stronger, but he'll be ready by the weekend. I hope you'll join me when I take him out."

"I wouldn't miss it for anything," I say with excitement. "I can't believe that he can spend so much time with humans and still be set free."

"At the end of the day, he's still a wild animal. He's hunted and lived wild his whole life. He won't have any problems readjusting to that."

"I'm glad." I blink as I feel myself tearing up. "Is it weird that it makes me a little sad to say goodbye to him?"

"It's not weird at all." Noah takes my hand and gives it a squeeze. "It's normal to get a little attached. If we didn't care, we wouldn't be doing the work."

"Speaking of being proud," I say, clearing my throat. "I'm *so* proud of you, Noah. Spread Your Wings is important and wonderful."

"Now you're going to make me blush."

"Well, it's true. I think you're amazing."

"Do you think I'm sexy?"

I tip my head, looking him over as if I have to *really* think about it.

"Yeah, I guess that's a good word."

"Hot?"

"Oh, Lord, you just want me to feed your ego."

He grins and pulls me out of my chair, leaving our dirty dishes on the table.

"I have more for you," he informs me.

"More than dinner?"

"Oh, yeah. That was just the beginning."

He leads me back to the bedroom.

"Sit on the bed for a minute."

I comply and watch as he rushes into the bathroom, turns on the tap in the tub, then rushes back out to the kitchen. Thirty seconds later, he returns holding a lit candle and something tucked under his arm.

"Almost ready," he says as he hurries by.

He makes two more trips to the kitchen and then walks to me with a laugh.

"That was far sexier in my head."

"Actually, it was fun to watch you bustle about. It was cute."

"Cute?" He scowls down at me. "Take that back."

"No way, you're the cutest."

He leans in and plants his lips next to my ear. "I'll show you how *un*cute I am in about thirty minutes."

He leads me into the bathroom, and I sigh in pleasure. The tub is full of steaming water and smells like lavender and frankincense, my favorite. Candles are lit, wine is ready for me, and there's a bowl of pistachio ice cream on the tray that sits across the soaking tub.

"This is ridiculously pretty."

"Soak. Relax. Enjoy. I'll come get you in a bit."

He closes the door behind him, and I hurry out of my clothes, excited to be pampered.

And pampered I am! The wine and ice cream, the hot water, the oils. It's decadent.

Sometime later, I've finished the ice cream, the glass of wine, and I'm leaning back and letting my mind float aimlessly when Noah returns.

I don't open my eyes, but I can hear him and feel the shift in the energy in the room. It's always more intense when Noah's near.

"You look happy."

"So happy."

He dips his fingers into the water. "It's getting cold."

"Don't care." He chuckles as I open my eyes and smile up at him. "Thank you."

"You're welcome." He takes my hand and pulls me up, helps me out of the tub, and wraps me in a huge, fluffy towel, careful to dry me completely. His eyes travel over my skin as he wipes the terrycloth over it. "You're so soft. So smooth."

His hands glide down my arms, and the next thing I know, I'm in his hold, and he's carrying me to the bedroom where more candles are lit. He brought the bouquet of flowers in and set them on the bedside table on my side of the bed.

"You're not cute," I say as I trace the line of his jaw. "You're sexy. Hot. The hottest."

"Now you're getting it," he says with a grin as he lays me down on the bed. "But you? Holy shit, Fal."

He presses a wet kiss just below my sternum, above my navel. His hands cradle my hips, his fingertips gripping my skin firmly. Pure sensation pulses through me.

And he hasn't even touched me *there*.

"Goosebumps," he murmurs as he kisses below my navel now. "I must be doing my job."

"Holy shit," I mutter, my legs scissoring in anticipation. He spreads my legs, nudging his shoulders between my thighs, and groans at the sight before him.

"Jesus, babe." He drags one finger down the center of my pubis, lightly over my clit, and down into my wet folds. "You make me crazy. You put me on my goddamn knees."

He leans in and licks from my lips to my clit, and I have to hold my breath as my entire body tenses.

"It's never been like this," he says before covering my core with his mouth and sucking in little pulsing motions, sending me right over the edge into oblivion.

When I come down to Earth, he's nudging his jeans down his hips and reaches over his head to pull off his shirt without even unbuttoning it. He tosses it aside and braces himself on either side of my shoulders, dropping down to kiss me, intoxicating me with his musky scent, his firm lips, his hard cock pressing against my center.

"You're everything," he whispers against my lips. I can smell myself on him, and it only intensifies my hunger for him. "You're everything good in my life, Fallon."

With those words, he presses inside me, pushing until he's balls-deep, making us both sigh in pleasure.

Being with Noah is different from anything I've ever experienced before. It's like taking a clean, deep breath for the first time in my life. Not that I couldn't breathe before, but with him, it's different. It's easier.

I fist his hair, holding on as we ride out the need we have for each other until we're a panting, heaving pair of bodies, spent from passion.

"Mine," he says between breaths. "All mine."

* * * *

Maybe evening classes weren't the best idea I've ever had.

Or, maybe it's just time to finally hire another instructor to take the late-day classes for me. I'm up so early in the morning that by eight in the evening, I'm completely wrecked. It makes for a long day, and even though it's just twice a week, it's throwing off my schedule more than I anticipated.

Tomorrow is Friday, and Noah asked me to go with him to set my eagle free in the afternoon. I'm both excited and dreading it. I don't want to say goodbye to him, but that's selfish of me. He *needs* to go live his eagle life.

The sun has gone down, and it's that time of day when driving isn't ideal. The lighting is odd, casting shadows and making it difficult to see even with the headlights. With the beams in my rearview mirror from the person behind me, it's even worse.

I squint, certain I see something up ahead on the road, but when I get closer, it's just a shadow.

"Yeah, maybe evening classes aren't going to work for me," I mumble.

I sigh and brush some hair off my face, and three deer dart onto the highway, right in front of me. I crank the wheel to the right, trying to avoid them, and the Jeep jerks into the gravel on the shoulder of the road. Suddenly, I'm falling down the embankment to the pasture below.

When the Jeep stops, head-first into a tree, I freeze, staring through a shattered windshield.

My insides scream in pain, and my head hurts. I reach up to touch it and come away with sticky blood on my fingers.

I reach over for my phone, but it's nowhere to be found.

"Oh my God," I croak. "How am I going to call for help?"

I wince, more pain searing through me.

"Hello?"

Someone's here!

A flashlight shines in my eyes, making me scowl.

"Fallon! Fuck, Fallon. I've called the ambulance."

"Who are you?"

I don't even recognize my own voice.

"Sam," he says soothingly. His hands move over me gently. "I'm checking for anything that's broken. Where do you hurt?"

"Inside," I say, finding it hard to catch my breath.

"Inside your body?"

"Yeah."

"Arms and legs?"

I shake my head. "No. I don't think so."

We can hear sirens coming in the distance.

"Oh my God, am I going to die?"

"No," Sam says firmly and holds my hand. "No way, help is coming."

"I want Noah."

"I'll call him after we get you loaded into the ambulance."

There's commotion around us. Voices.

Loud voices.

"Down here!" Sam yells. "One patient. Possible internal injuries. Head laceration. No extremity fractures that I can see."

It feels like everything moves in slow motion as I'm unbuckled from my seat and moved by four men to a flat board, strapped on, and carried up the embankment to the ambulance.

"Where's Sam?" I ask weakly.

"Right here," he says, retaking my hand. "I'm not leaving you, honey."

"Call Noah."

"Yes, ma'am."

"Blood pressure is low," someone says.

"Noah, it's Sam. I need to let you know that I'm in an ambulance with Fallon. Yeah, she was in a car accident. I was driving behind her."

So it was *his* lights blinding me in the rearview.

"I don't know what the injuries are. She's conscious, and that's good. Yeah, we'll meet you there."

"Is he coming?"

"He is." Sam leans over me so I can see him. "He's going to meet us there. You just relax and let these people help you, okay?"

"'Kay. Getting sleepy."

"Don't sleep," Sam says, frowning down at me. "Not until we get you to a doctor. Okay? Stay with me, Fallon."

"Okay." I wince. "My insides really hurt."

"Internal injuries," someone says.

"Are we almost there?" I ask.

"Yep, we're turning in now. Keep those pretty green eyes open for us, okay? Just a few more minutes."

I try to nod and feel the ambulance come to a stop. The back doors are flung open, and I'm wheeled out of the vehicle and inside the hospital where people are hurrying about.

"Fallon McCarthy," someone says. "What room?"

"Three. The doctor's in there."

I'm taken into a room, and when the doctor is satisfied that I don't have a broken spine, I'm moved to a hospital bed.

"Oh God," I moan.

"You got beat up pretty good." A man smiles at me. "I'm Dr. Merritt. I'm a surgeon, and I'm here in case you need surgery."

"I don't know if I do."

"Let's find out."

Chapter Eighteen

~Noah~

"Where the fuck is she?" I demand as I burst through the doors of the emergency room. "Where is Fallon?"

"Hey," Sam says as he jogs to me. "She's with the doctors now. It'll just be a few minutes before you can go in."

"What in the hell happened?"

"She was driving ahead of me, and she seemed fine. I mean, nothing looked out of the ordinary. But some deer ran onto the highway in front of her, and she swerved, lost control of the Jeep, and slid down the embankment into a tree."

"Fuck." I rub my hand over my mouth, a cold sweat on my skin.

"She never lost consciousness, which is a good sign, like I said. She has some pain, but who wouldn't after that?"

"Yeah." I nod. "Yeah, that's true."

"There." Sam points to a room as Dr. Merritt comes out of it and walks straight to us. "This is Noah, Fallon's boyfriend."

"Hi, Drake." I shake his hand. I'd seen Drake around town since he moved here a couple of years ago. "How is she?"

"You can come in," he says, gesturing for us to follow him. We walk inside, and I hurry to Fallon's side, taking her hand in mine.

"Oh, baby." She has a bandage over her eye, and some bruising on her neck where the seatbelt hit.

"Hey," she says weakly. "Something happened."

"She's actually very lucky," Drake says. "We don't see any broken bones. She's very banged up, but so far, no collapsed lungs or anything else to raise flags. She's going to be here for a few days while we keep an eye on her in case that changes."

"She can stay for as long as it takes," I say, watching her frown. "What is it, babe?"

"Hurts," she says. "My Jeep is totaled."

"We'll get you another one," I assure her. "The important thing is that you're okay."

"Not okay," she murmurs. Her eyes are closed. "Have to turn the eagle loose."

"We can do that later. Maybe she should sleep," I say, and Drake nods his head.

"She'll need plenty of rest and fluids, and we'll start an IV antibiotic as well to combat any possible infection. We'll keep a close eye on her."

"I'm staying," I say firmly, not willing to leave her side.

"She'll feel better knowing you're here," Drake says with a smile. "I'm sorry this happened, Noah. I don't know what I'd do if it was Abby."

I nod, watching Fallon. She's frowning.

"What is it, love?"

"Something's wrong," she says again. The monitors start to go crazy.

"Out," Drake says, all business again as more people rush into the room.

"Come on," Sam says, tugging my arm. "Give them room."

I step back, and a nurse pushes us out of the room altogether and pulls a curtain so we can't see what's happening.

"Code blue, room three," comes over the intercom.

"What the fuck does that mean?" I look to Sam, whose face is white and hard. "What does it mean, Sam?"

"A code blue means she has no pulse."

I pace away, scrubbing my hands down my face. I faintly hear Sam calling Gray through the rushing in my ears. More people hustle in and out of Fallon's room, and the next thing I know, she's being wheeled away, a whole team of people surrounding her.

"Drake!" I yell. "What's happening?"

He doesn't even spare me a glance as he runs alongside her bed and disappears through a heavy set of double doors.

"You can wait in the waiting room," the nurse says. "We will update you when we know more."

"What in the hell is going on?" I ask, but she can only shake her head.

"We don't know. Her heart is beating again, but they've taken her in for exploratory surgery to find out what's happening. That's all I know. Dr. Merritt will come and talk to you when he's done."

She walks away, and I follow Sam to the waiting room on numb legs and collapse on a chair, my head falling into my hands.

Sam's talking on the phone next to me. I can't hear the words. I don't give a shit what he's saying. I need to know if Fallon's going to live through this nightmare. I can't lose her. Not now, not when I just found her.

"We're here."

My head whips up at the sound of my mom's voice.

"I called them," Sam says, patting me on the shoulder. "You need family. I'm going to head home, but I'd appreciate it if someone could let me know how she's doing."

"We will," Dad says.

"Thank you," I say, standing and shaking Sam's hand. "If you hadn't been there—"

"I was," he says with a nod. "No need to think about the alternative. Keep me posted."

He leaves, and I'm left with Mom and Dad. Autumn joins us.

"Gray's talking with Sam," she says, her eyes wide with fear and concern. "What happened?"

When Gray joins us, I tell them what I know. Fallon's accident, her injuries, and her coding before being swept off to surgery.

"Scared the hell out of me," I mumble, pushing my hands through my hair. "I don't know what's happening back there."

"Waiting is always the hardest part," Dad says grimly. "Dr. Merritt is the best there is. She's in excellent hands."

I nod and sit again, sick to my stomach with worry. I wish I was back there. I wish I could see what's happening.

* * * *

"It's been three hours," I mutter in frustration.

"That doesn't mean it's bad news," Mom says, but she doesn't make me feel any better.

"I know who I can call." I pull out my phone and call Brad Hull.

"Hull."

"I need your wife," I tell him. "Fallon's in surgery, and Hannah's a doctor. She can get me information. Better than that, you're the chief of police. Get your ass down here and demand to be filled in on Fallon's status."

"Whoa," Brad says. "Slow down. Was Fallon the accident on the highway earlier tonight?"

"Yes, and she's been in surgery for hours. I need information. I'm going crazy."

"Noah."

I glance up to find Drake walking toward us.

"Never mind, Drake's here." I hang up and hurry to the doctor. "Tell me she's alive."

"She's alive," he says and sighs. He has bags under his eyes as if he hasn't slept in a week. "She's out of surgery. She had a lacerated spleen and was bleeding out."

"Jesus," Gray mutters as my mom gasps.

"We have the bleeding under control, and I stitched her up. We had to give her a transfusion. She'll be okay."

"When can I see her?"

"She's in recovery now, but she'll be in a room within the hour, and you can be with her." He shakes my hand. "I'll be here all night, just to keep an eye on her."

"How long have you been here?" I ask him.

He checks the time. "Going on eighteen hours now."

"Thank you. I mean that."

"Like I said, I don't know what I'd do if it was Abby. I'll stay through the night." He nods and leaves, and I fold Mom in a tight hug.

"Thank God she's okay," she says.

"I need to see her," I reply and nod in agreement. "But I'm relieved. You guys don't have to stay. I'll let you know if there's any change."

"We love her," Autumn says and wipes a tear from her eye. "We all love her."

"I know."

Once the family leaves, another new nurse comes to get me and leads me down a long hallway, past a nurses' station, to Fallon's room. She's hooked up to more machines, but she's breathing on her own.

"Can I stay the night?" I ask quietly. "I'm her only family."

"I don't see why not," the nurse says with a smile. "Just let her rest."

I nod and pull up a chair beside Fallon, sit in it, and take her hand in mine. It's cold.

I kiss the knuckles, and for the first time in a long time, I pray to whoever's listening that she makes it through this okay. She has to.

Six months ago…hell, *two* months ago, I didn't know that someone could come to mean so much. That the thought of being without them was like ripping my heart from my chest.

I study Fallon for a long time, watch her breathing in and out. The monitors beep rhythmically. The lights are dim. Finally, I let myself drift to sleep.

* * * *

My neck is killing me.

I wake up and glance around, confused for a brief second, but it all immediately comes flooding back.

My neck hurts because I slept in the chair with my head resting on the bed next to Fallon's hip.

She hasn't moved. That worries me.

The nurse that led me in here walks in and checks the monitors.

"Should she still be asleep?" I ask.

"It's not unheard of," she says. "She'll wake up in a little while. Her body went through quite the trauma. She's healing."

She smiles and then walks out, and I'm left alone with the love of my life.

"Good morning," I murmur softly. "You scared me, baby. More like terrified, actually."

I sigh and kiss her hand. It flexes slightly.

"You're listening."

Her lips move, but she doesn't say anything.

"You just rest, and I'll talk." I reach up and brush a piece of hair off her bruised cheek. Now that I really look, she has more bruises that showed up through the night—on her shoulders, her face, and her arms. "God, Fal, that Jeep kicked your ass."

"Yeah," she whispers. "Hurts."

A wave of relief courses through me at the sound of her weak voice.

"I can ask them to give you more medicine."

"No. Don't want to sleep." She licks her lips and opens one eye, searching for me. "Love you."

"God, I love you, too." Tears threaten, but I don't give a shit. "You almost left me last night."

"Didn't mean to."

"I know." I swallow hard. "Fal, we talked about this, remember? Whether it's moving out of state or dying on me, you're not leaving. It's just not happening."

"Bossy."

I swipe at a tear and smile at her. "Yeah, I'm bossy. You can't leave just when it's getting good around here. We have *so much* to do together, honey. There are thousands of amazing days ahead of us, and you're not going to cheat me out of them, you hear me?"

She squeezes my hand three times.

"Not going anywhere."

"Good." It feels so damn good to hear her voice. "Are you cold?"

"Cold. Hurts."

"I know. Let's get you more medicine."

"'Kay."

I press the red call button and let the nurse know that Fallon's awake, cold, and in pain.

"We can fix that," she says with a smile. "I'll be right back."

She returns with a couple of warm blankets, a new bag of liquid to hook up to Fallon's IV, and then pulls a bottle and a syringe out of her rolling cart after entering something on the computer.

"This will help, but she'll sleep some more."

"She needs to sleep," I reply. "I'll be right here, baby."

* * * *

"I've been in here for a week," Fallon says. "I'm ready to go home." And thank God for it.

"Do you remember the part where you almost died?" Drake asks her. "Because I do. Trust me, we're all ready to get you out of here."

"Am I a pain in the butt?"

Drake laughs. "Yes, actually."

"Good. Send me *home*. I have an eagle to set loose, and a business to run."

Drake looks at me, but I just shrug. "I got nothin'. But I do love seeing her sassy like this as opposed to where she was a week ago."

"Agreed."

"Awesome. So, if you're done talking about me like I'm not here, I'll just get dressed and—"

"You don't have any clothes," I remind her. "They had to be cut off you."

"I don't mind going home in this," she says, frowning. The bruises on her face have faded from bright purple to a yellow-green. "I've peed and pooped on my own, I can walk, and my incision is healing. What more do you want from me?"

"You're right," Drake says, surprising her. "You can go home today."

"You're not playing with my emotions, right?" Fallon asks.

"No, I'm not. Let me get the discharge paperwork together, and we'll spring you. You need to follow up with me in a week."

"I can do that."

"And you can't work during that week."

She deflates. "I'm *so bored.*"

"Healing is boring work," he says with a shrug. "No working. I mean it. I had my hands in your abdomen a week ago. It's a big deal, Fallon."

"Okay. At least I can be bored at home."

"There's the spirit. The nurse will be back with your discharge paperwork, and I'll see you in a week."

He leaves, and Fallon smiles at me. "I'm going home."

"Seems so," I say, not admitting to her that Drake told me this morning she'd be able to go home. I've had helpers at the house today, getting it ready for her.

"No hovering once we're there," she says, pointing her finger at me. "You've been here all week. You need to get back to work, too."

"I have more volunteers than I know what to do with," I remind her. "Besides, you're the most important thing. Always."

She smiles softly, then winces. "This damn black eye still smarts. Anyway, we need to go back to some normalcy."

"We'll get there," I assure her. "Let's just worry about getting you healed up, and then we'll find normal."

"Sounds great to me."

Chapter Nineteen

~Fallon~

I feel like I've been...well, like I hit a tree. It hurts worse than I let on to Noah, but he's been worried enough over the past week. He's been with me every minute of every day, until last night when I encouraged him to go home and get some sleep. He can't help me if he's exhausted.

I was shocked when he agreed.

Dr. Merritt assured me this morning before Noah arrived at the hospital that the soreness is normal, and as long as I take it easy, I'll start to feel better each day.

"Where's my Jeep?" I ask Noah as he pulls into the driveway in front of the house.

"It was towed to a salvage yard," he replies with a grim sigh. "I'm sorry, sweetheart."

"Did they get my purse and stuff?"

"Yes, it's inside," he replies, cutting the engine. "Don't move. I'll come around and help you."

"No argument here," I say with a smile. I may be stubborn, but I'm not stupid. He circles his SUV and opens my door, but rather than help me down to my feet, he scoops me into his arms, easily lifting me from the vehicle. "Having a super strong boyfriend is so handy."

His lips tip up in a grin. "I'll keep up with my workouts, just for you."

I laugh and lean my head on his shoulder as he easily carries me up the steps to the front door. It's unlocked, and when we step inside, I'm assaulted by something that smells amazing.

"What's that?"

"Soup," he says with a grin. "Mom and Autumn have been here all day, getting the house ready for you. Mom made her special chicken noodle soup. It's guaranteed to help you feel better."

"The smell alone has already done that." He takes me back to the bedroom and sets me gingerly on the bed, on top of the covers. "I'd like to change out of this godforsaken hospital gown."

"On it," he says and walks to the dresser, finding a pair of yoga shorts and a loose T-shirt. I move to the edge of the bed, and Noah helps me untie the gown. "I'm going to burn this."

"I want to help."

Before he passes me my clothes, his eyes take inventory of the injuries still healing, and his lips flatten in a grim line.

"Jesus, Fal."

"It looks worse than it feels."

His eyes find mine. "Don't bullshit me."

"Okay, it hurts. I'm sore. But it's getting better, and that's not a lie."

He helps me step into the shorts and gently tugs them up to my hips, then slips the tee over my head.

"Ah, that's already better. I'll tackle the shower later tonight. I don't think I have the energy for it now."

"You need to rest," he says, kissing my forehead. He helps me get settled back against a mountain of pillows and then pulls a rolling tray I haven't seen before over beside me.

"Did you buy a hospital tray?" I ask.

"No, Nancy and Jeff had it from when they took care of my grandparents. It's on loan for a couple of days."

"It makes me feel old," I say, wrinkling my nose. "But also grateful. Thank you. Also, I don't think that TV was there before."

"Good eye," he says. "Gray and Autumn bought it for you."

"Wow, that was nice of them." I stare at the black screen for a moment, overwhelmed by the love Noah's family has shown me.

"Do you need to sleep right now, or are you up for some more gifts?"

I scowl. "Why on earth would anyone get me gifts?"

"Because they love you," he says casually as if it's no big deal at all. "What do you say? Are you up for it?"

"Heck, yes."

He grins and kisses my head, then disappears from the room for a moment. When Noah returns, he has gift bags and even a few shipping boxes.

"Holy shit, Noah."

"There's a lot of love in my hands," he says with a chuckle. "Let's start with the shipping boxes. I have a knife."

He pulls out his pocketknife and slices the tape on the boxes, then sits them next to me.

I pull the card out of the first one and smile. "This is from Penny. Shit, I haven't called her."

"Willa did," he replies. "Obviously."

"Right." Noah has to help me pull the wrapped box out, and I smile widely when I unwrap it. "A new essential oils diffuser. Oh, this is beautiful. I've wanted to get one for our bedroom. It's perfect."

"We'll get it all set up when you're done," he says, setting it aside. Before me, Noah probably didn't give a rat's ass about essential oils, but he doesn't even think twice about me incorporating them into our home.

He's amazing.

The second shipping box is from Lacey, which also surprises me. "Whoa."

"She was worried sick," Noah says, watching me open the gift. "She asked me to call her every day. She really loves you, Fal."

"Yeah," I whisper, running my fingers over the soft faux fur of the slippers she sent me. "These are so soft. This is thoughtful of her."

Noah sets the boxes on the floor next to the bed and passes me a half dozen gift bags.

"This is crazy," I mutter, but by the time I've opened them all, I'm teary-eyed. Noah's parents got me a new robe that matches the slippers Lacey sent. Gray and Autumn gave me a subscription to Netflix so I can comfortably binge on the new TV, and the rest of the family sent snacks and little things to keep me occupied. "It's too much."

"We're not done," he says with a laugh. "But for the last thing, we'll have to go outside."

I stare at him for a moment, completely overwhelmed. "Noah."

"Come on. I'll carry you if you're up for it."

"Is there another surprise party out there? Because I'm *not* feeling up for that. I might split my incision open from crying too much."

"No, no one's here but you and me." He kisses my head. "What do you say?"

"Let's do this, and then I'll sleep for a week."

He lifts me and carries me out the back door onto the deck, and I can only stare, sure I'm seeing things.

"Am I still under anesthesia?" I whisper.

"No."

"Noah, that's a brand new Jeep with a red ribbon on the hood."

"That it is," he says as he sits in a chair and cuddles me in his lap. "We'll go check it out later, but I wanted to show you."

"You didn't have to—"

"I didn't," he says. "At least, not by myself. The whole family, including the Hulls, went in on it."

I stare at him, too shocked to cry. "Are you telling me that Josh and Zack, your parents, Jeff and Nancy, Gray and Autumn, Brad and Hannah—"

"Christian and Jenna and Max and Willa," he finishes, nodding. "Even Lacey helped. All of us, babe."

"But." I stare at the bright red Jeep with the top off, gleaming in the afternoon sunshine.

"But what?"

"But it's too much," I finish with a whisper.

"No," he says, pressing his lips to my temple. "No, it's not. We love you, *so much.*"

"I can never repay them for this."

"Family doesn't ask to be paid back," he says. "And that's what you have here, Fallon. A big family."

* * * *

"I feel guilty that he's had to wait for me," I admit a few days later as Noah drives us over to Spread Your Wings. "He should already be free."

"And he will be, today," Noah says, taking it easy over the bumps in the gravel road. "Are you okay?"

"I'm fine," I assure him. I have my appointment with Dr. Merritt in just two days, and I've been improving every day. The rest has helped, but I'm ready to be *out* of bed.

Noah pulls into a parking space and hurries around to my side of the car to help me out. He finally stopped carrying me around yesterday.

"Are you sure you don't want me to carry you?"

"I have to walk, Noah. I'm not an invalid." I shake my head and gingerly walk beside him to the building housing my eagle. "I'm just slow."

"Slow is fine; we're not in a hurry." He rests his hand on the small of my back and patiently walks with me down the row of cages to my favorite one.

"Hey there, handsome boy," I croon to the bird. He perks up, his head tilting, and he flaps his wings. "Well, look at that, showing off your healed wing. Good boy."

"He's happy to see you," Noah says with a smile.

"I'm happy to see him, too. I'm sorry I was away for so long, buddy."

There's already a carrier in the cage, and Noah quickly gets the eagle safely inside, then carries him out to the truck. I do need help getting into the passenger seat, but then we're off to let the eagle go.

"Where are we going?"

"Back where you found him. Or close to it since you can't exactly climb a mountain today."

"No, not today."

He drives to the trailhead and parks, and we walk with the bird down the trail a ways until it starts to veer up.

"Looks like this is the place," Noah says, setting the carrier on a stump and opening the door. "We just wait for him to fly away."

"I'm going to talk to him since this is how we started."

"Go right ahead."

Noah steps away, and I approach the open carrier. "Hey, baby. You get to go home today."

The eagle hops out of the carrier then flaps his wings and perches on top of it, looking at me. I pet his head, loving the soft feel of his feathers.

"That's right, you're free to go. You're all healed up." I feel tears prick my eyes. "I'm *so* glad I found you that day. It changed both of our lives."

He cocks his head to the side, watching me as if he's listening and understanding every word.

"I don't think I can ever thank you enough," I say and smile when he squawks. "Well, you're welcome. You go live your life now, okay? Do you have a lady friend? Do eagles mate for life?"

"They do," Noah says softly.

"Go find your girl and have some babies. Go soar high, sweet boy."

He tilts his head, squawks, and flies up into a nearby tree, looking around. Noah takes the carrier away and stows it in the truck, and when he returns, I'm sitting on the stump, watching the eagle.

"He's not leaving."

"He's getting his bearings," Noah says softly, sitting next to me on the stump. "He's a gorgeous bird."

"He really is. Did you see the mark on his beak?"

"He must have been in a fight at some point," Noah says with a nod.

"How are the owlets we found doing?" I ask, making conversation while we watch.

"They're getting big. You should come see them. I think we'll let them go in about a week, as well."

"Oh, that's wonderful. They'll know what to do?"

"What, be owls?"

"Well, yeah."

"They will. We've been working with them in the flight barn. They're going to be great."

I sigh and lean into him, resting my head on his shoulder. "I love your job."

"I'm rather fond of it myself," he says with a laugh. "And I'm glad you like it. You're welcome to help out whenever you want."

"Good, because I like it a lot. I want to learn more."

"What, with all of your spare time?"

I shrug a shoulder. "We make time for important things."

He kisses my head. "We should go home."

"I want to wait until he flies away."

And so we do, sitting on the stump as hikers pass by, looking up to see what we're looking at and then moving on.

Finally, after about thirty minutes, the eagle squawks once more.

"Goodbye, friend," I say and watch as he spreads his wings and soars away.

"Why are you crying?" Noah asks, catching a tear with his fingertip.

"I'm not." I sniff. "I'm happy."

"You don't look happy."

"I'm happy for him," I clarify. "But I'm going to miss him."

"There will be more birds that need help."

"But none like him."

Chapter Twenty

~Fallon~

Eight weeks.

It's been eight weeks since the accident. Since I almost lost my life and I said goodbye to the eagle.

So much has happened.

Amazing, beautiful, *big* things.

But the biggest of them all is happening in about ten minutes.

"Don't be nervous," Noah says in my ear.

"How can I not be?" I ask, taking a deep breath. "It's sink or swim time."

"You're going to swim like an Olympian," he says with a wink.

I pray he's right.

Tonight is the grand opening of my new yoga studio, *Asana*. I've put a lot of blood, sweat, and tears into the place, and I'm finally ready to unleash it on the community of Cunningham Falls.

My community.

I don't think I could be more excited—or more scared.

"Are you ready?" Autumn asks. She helped me plan this party, and I don't know what I would have done without her. "I think there are already people outside."

"I see them."

Once I took over the building, the owner of the ski shop decided to relocate his business, so I moved into the entire space. It was better for my business, but way more work for Gray, who didn't disappoint.

"Let's open up," I announce, clapping my hands. I unlock the door and open it wide. "Come on in, everyone!"

"This is *gorgeous*," Willa says, accepting a glass of champagne from a server as she steps in the door. "Oh, Fallon, I love it. I'll never miss a class."

"You've barely seen it," I say, laughing.

"And I love what I see. I'm going to wander around."

"Please do. There are two small studios upstairs, and lots to see, so feel free to check it all out."

It feels like half of Cunningham Falls files through my door, and an hour into the grand opening, the space is full.

"I'm afraid we're a fire hazard," Gray says, chuckling as he joins me, passing me my first glass of champagne. "You've earned this."

"Thanks." I take a sip and smile as I survey the crowd. "Have you seen Noah?"

"He's around here somewhere," Gray replies and nods at someone across the room.

"Autumn throws one hell of a party. Her business is going to thrive."

"She's damn good," Gray agrees with a nod. "Speaking of, I'm going to check in on her, make sure she doesn't need anything."

"Sounds good. Thanks, Gray. You did a fantastic job."

He nods with a proud smile and walks away to find his fiancée.

"Are you selling these?" Brooke Henderson asks, pointing to the yoga mats rolled up on the wide shelves Gray made me.

"I am," I reply with a smile. "What color do you like best?"

The rest of the evening is more of the same, customers happy with what they see, and ready to buy merchandise or sign up for classes. Some do both.

It's proving to be a successful night, after all.

"This is absolutely the kind of place I want to learn to do yoga in," Mrs. Blakely says, flashing me a kind smile. "Sign me up."

"Oh, wonderful," I say, unable to suppress my happiness. "I think you'll love it."

"I do, too."

When ten o'clock rolls around, and it's time to close the doors, I'm exhausted in the best way possible.

"I don't think that could have gone better," Autumn says.

"It's a good thing I hired three more instructors," I say with a nod.

"I filled the classes. There will likely be some no-shows and drop-offs in the first few weeks, but as of right now, we're full."

"Amazing," Noah says behind me, and I whirl at the sound of his voice.

"There you are. Where have you been? I've been looking for you."

"I was here the whole time." His face looks innocent enough, but I narrow my eyes at him.

"I didn't see you."

"There were a lot of people here," Gray says with a shrug. "And you were busy. Probably just missed each other."

"I suppose you're right." I hug Autumn and Gray. "Thank you, *so* much. I'll be calling you for all of my remodeling or party-planning needs."

"We're happy to help," Autumn says before she and Gray take their leave.

"I'm ready to go home." I walk through the space and turn off all of the lights. "I have a cleaning crew coming in the morning."

"Perfect," Noah says, holding his hand out for mine. "Let's go."

We walk out the back door into the alley where Noah's SUV is parked. I haven't driven at night since the accident. I know that as time passes, I'll feel more confident about it, but for now, there's no need. I've hired instructors to cover the evening classes, and Noah's always happy to take me anywhere I want or need to go.

"It was better than I expected," I gush once we're on the highway, headed toward the house. "I honestly wasn't anticipating that kind of turnout."

"People are curious, especially in a small town," Noah replies. "Of course, they want to come see what you've done. Not to mention, it's right on Main, and the building's been covered in a tarp while Gray's crew worked."

"I wanted to create a mystery." I sigh, sitting back in the seat. Summer is over, and we're officially into fall. It's still beautiful during the day, but the nights are cooler. "And I guess it worked."

"It was a great idea. And the building *looks* different, so it wasn't a disappointment."

"It's amazing what some paint and elbow grease will do."

We're quiet for the rest of the drive. I'm exhausted and energized at the same time. I feel like I could both sleep for a month and run a marathon.

It's taken me the whole two months since the accident to get back to my pre-injury health. It was amazing to me how quickly I lost muscle tone, flexibility, and muscle memory. But with dedication and hard work, I'm back to where I was before.

"It's amazing how we lose the sunlight so quickly now," I say, watching Noah's high-beams illuminate the road to the house. "Three months ago, it would have still been light outside."

"You're right," he says. "I'm not quite ready for winter."

"We have a little time before the snow flies."

He nods and parks in front of the house.

"Why don't you ever use the garage?" I ask, pointing to the detached three-car garage not far from the house.

"I do in the winter," he says. "I guess I'm just lazy in the summer. Why do you ask?"

"Just curious." I shrug and follow him inside. "I'm going to take a shower."

"Why don't we do a little stargazing first?" he asks, taking my hand in his and kissing my knuckles. "I want some more time with you. I had to share you all evening."

I cock my head to the side, feeling a shift in the energy but unable to put my finger on why.

"Okay." We walk outside, and I gasp, stopping in my tracks. "Oh, this is pretty."

Noah has strung twinkle lights above and around the deck. Rose petals are sprinkled everywhere, and champagne is chilling in a bucket by the chairs.

"Noah."

I turn to find him smiling, his hands in his pockets as if he's nervous.

"We need to celebrate," he says simply and leads me to a chair. "Have a seat."

"Are these chocolate-covered strawberries?"

He nods and pours me a glass of champagne, does the same for himself, and then sits next to me. The chairs are angled more, so I'm looking right at him, our knees almost touching.

"You know, I didn't want to fall in love, Fallon. It really wasn't in the plan. I had my business, my family, and I was content.

"Or, at least I thought I was."

He frowns, staring at his glass.

"But then you came into my life, and I started to want more. To want everything."

He looks up at me now, and I hold my breath, listening intently.

"I love you so much it hurts." He swallows hard. "I ache with it, and I don't want to ease that ache. I look at you, and I see everything good in my life. I'm all in, Fallon, for the rest of my days. I want to grow old with you, sitting on this deck and watching the sun rise over the mountains. I want babies—when you're ready."

I feel my lips twitch, remembering my awkward conversation on this very deck about children.

"I want to enjoy my community, my family, and I want it all with you."

He sets his glass aside and slips down onto one knee. I gasp, covering my mouth with my hand and holding his gaze with mine. He holds out a diamond ring that sparkles in the twinkling lights.

"Fallon, will you marry me?"

"God, yes!" I throw my arms around his neck, holding on tightly. I press my lips to his ear. "I love you so much, Noah King."

He eases back and slips the ring on my finger, then kisses the knuckle above it. I feel the zing of electricity all the way up my arm.

I lean in, cupping his cheeks, and kiss him, firmly at first, but then the tone changes to soft and sensual. My nipples tighten. My core flexes.

"If you're going to be my husband, does that mean I can get you naked whenever I want?"

He cocks a brow, interest filling his brown eyes. "That's always been the case, sweetheart."

"Oh, good."

I tug up his shirt, but he stills my hands. "Hold that thought. There's no one out here, but just in case."

He hurries over and unplugs the twinkle lights, and we're just in moonlight now. He pulls his shirt over his head and tosses it aside as he joins me.

"Is it too cold to do this out here?" I ask.

"You tell me. You make me so hot, I could do this in sub-zero temperatures."

I laugh and reach for the waistband of his jeans.

"I'm hot for you," I answer honestly, and he leans in to plant a kiss on my forehead, in that way he does that has set me on fire since our first date. "Let's get you out of these clothes."

"If I'd known a proposal got you this turned on, I would have done it a month ago," he says, tugging my dress over my head and cursing under his breath when he has me naked. "God, I love the way you look. Especially in the moonlight."

"I have a scar," I say, as he traces the line with his fingertip.

"It'll fade," he whispers before kissing it sweetly. "And it's a reminder that you survived, Fal."

"Yeah, I did." I grin as my hand plunges into his pants, encircling his already hard cock. "And thank goodness, because I want to be able to do this for the rest of my life."

I lean in and circle the tip with my tongue, then sink down, sucking hard.

"Fucking hell," he mutters, his hands planted in my hair. "Oh God, babe. I need you to stop doing that so I don't come in your mouth."

But I don't stop, so he picks me up and sits with me straddling him.

"Tonight is not for that," he says, pushing my hair over my shoulder. "It's for this."

He guides my hips up, and I sink over him, sighing in pleasure as he fills me.

His fingers tighten on my hips. He leans in to suck an already puckered nipple, and we move together under the stars, making silent promises to each other in the moonlight.

* * * *

"Did you get up early to clean up?" I ask as I sit on the deck with my tea. Noah beat me out here, a coffee mug in his hand and a smile on his handsome face.

"I couldn't sleep," he admits. "I think I'm too excited."

"You're sweet." I set my mug on the table between us and take a deep breath. "I can smell the change in the season."

"It's chilly this morning," he says and grins. "But you're warm in that robe."

"All of the gifts I got after the accident will come in handy all winter," I agree, warm in my slippers and robe. The sun is just about to come up over the mountains. The sky is purple and blue, and I'm content in the knowledge that I get to watch this sunrise every morning for the rest of my life.

Suddenly, a bald eagle lands on the railing of the deck, surprising us both.

"Wow," I whisper, and then frown. "Wait. Is that—?"

"It absolutely is," Noah breathes. "Look at the beak."

"It's my eagle," I say, leaning forward. "Hey there, sweet boy. How on earth did you find us?"

"They're smarter than we give them credit for," Noah says. "He likes you."

The eagle watches me, tilting his head as we talk.

"I like you, too," I say and hold my hand up for him to see. "You get to be the first to know. Noah asked me to marry him."

The eagle squawks, making both Noah and me chuckle. Another eagle lands in the maple tree about twenty feet away.

"Looks like he's got a sweetheart," I say and smile at the eagle. "Good for you, buddy. Are you going to make your home here?"

He squawks once more and flies over to the other bird.

"Me, too."

Epilogue

~Fallon~

Christmas Day

"I'm coming in there," Noah says and barges into the bathroom.

"I can't pee with you in here," I complain.

"You're not peeing on that stick without me," he says, shaking his head. "We're in this together."

"Can't we be in this together *after* I've peed?"

"No." He kisses my forehead as I rip open the box. "Jesus, how many did you buy?"

"Four. Just in case."

"In case there are four babies?"

I sigh. "No, in case one of them is wrong."

"But it's their whole purpose in life to be *right*," he says. "Wait. Did you get the ones that say *pregnant* or *not pregnant*?"

"No, I got the ones that have a line or no line. We're intelligent people, Noah. We can figure this out. Besides, aren't you a doctor?"

He stares at me like I've just announced I'm climbing Kilimanjaro.

"I'm a zoologist," he says. "I'm not a people doctor."

"Still, you're smart. We've got this."

"Okay, pee."

I scowl, unwrap the stick, pull off the cap, and shrug. "I guess I pee on this thing."

"Great. Let's do it."

"Why does the girl have to do it?" I wonder. "I mean, it's easier for men to aim."

"Because I'm not the one with a bun in the oven," he says with a laugh. "Come on, the suspense is killing me."

I sit on the toilet and stare at Noah as he leans on the vanity, his arms crossed over his chest, watching me intently.

"At least turn around. I can't do this with you watching me."

He sighs but complies, turning his back to me.

"You know, we've been married for a year," he reminds me. "I've already seen it all."

"You haven't seen me go to the bathroom," I say and tinkle on the stick. "Let's keep a few mysteries alive in our marriage."

"If that stick is positive, there will be few mysteries left," he says, and my stomach immediately erupts with butterflies.

"If it's positive," I say as I cap the stick and finish my job, then pull up my pants. "Everything is going to change."

"In wonderful ways," he says and turns when I flush and wash my hands. "How long do we wait?"

"Three minutes."

I set the test stick aside and walk into his arms, soaking him in. "What if it's negative?"

"We get to keep trying," he replies. "Today."

"I'm being serious."

"So am I, sweetheart. I can't keep my hands off of you."

I laugh and glance down. "Has it been three minutes?"

"No, it's been one minute."

"Well, that's all it took." I pick it up and grin. "Because this second line is as bright as can be."

"What does the second line mean?" He reaches for the box, but I take his hand in mine.

"We're having a baby."

He blinks as if the news is unexpected, which only makes me laugh.

"Uh, Noah? This happens when you *try* to get pregnant. Well, if you're lucky. And it seems we are."

"Holy shit." He grins and lifts me off my feet, spinning me in a circle. "Holy shit! We're having a baby!"

There's a knock on the door.

"Hello?" Gray calls out. "We want to open presents out here. Come on already."

We smile at each other. "We'd better go tell them."

"Why did we invite the whole family here for Christmas morning?" Noah asks. "I want to take you to bed and celebrate."

"Later." I open the door and smile up at Gray.

"Stop it with the Christmas hanky-panky already."

"Stop trying to ruin my fun," Noah counters as we walk out to the living room. Noah's parents came up from Arizona for the holiday, and even Lacey came from Portland. Gray and Autumn are passing out presents.

Noah raises a brow at me, but I shake my head.

Not yet.

Once all of the paper is torn, and we've gorged ourselves on cinnamon rolls and hot beverages, I nod at Noah.

"We have one more present," he says, taking my hand in his.

"We're having a baby," I announce.

"We know," Gray says, taking another cinnamon roll off the platter. "You were back there *forever.*"

"I listened in like any self-respecting mother does when she hears the words *pee on the stick*," Susan adds.

I look at Noah, and we dissolve into laughter.

"You didn't say anything!"

"We didn't want to ruin your announcement," Doug says as he pulls me in for a hug. "But I sure am happy, sweet girl."

"Looks like we'll be spending more time in the cabin," Susan agrees. "Because I'm *not* missing out on my grandchildren. What a blessing this is! Daughters *and* babies."

Autumn smiles, her hand on her swollen belly.

A blessing, not a burden.

That's what family is.

* * * *

Also from 1001 Dark Nights and Kristen Proby, discover Tempting Brooke, No Reservations, Easy With You, and Easy For Keeps.

Sign up for the 1001 Dark Nights Newsletter
and be entered to win a Tiffany Lock necklace.

There's a contest every quarter!

Go to www.1001DarkNights.com to subscribe.

As a bonus, all subscribers can download
FIVE FREE exclusive books!

Discover the Kristen Proby Crossover Collection

Soaring with Fallon: A Big Sky Novel
By Kristen Proby

Fallon McCarthy has climbed the corporate ladder. She's had the office with the view, the staff, and the plaque on her door. The unexpected loss of her grandmother taught her that there's more to life than meetings and conference calls, so she quit, and is happy to be a nomad, checking off items on her bucket list as she takes jobs teaching yoga in each place she lands in. She's happy being free, and has no interest in being tied down.

When Noah King gets the call that an eagle has been injured, he's not expecting to find a beautiful stranger standing vigil when he arrives. Rehabilitating birds of prey is Noah's passion, it's what he lives for, and he doesn't have time for a nosy woman who's suddenly taken an interest in Spread Your Wings sanctuary.

But Fallon's gentle nature, and the way she makes him laugh, and *feel* again draws him in. When it comes time for Fallon to move on, will Noah's love be enough for her to stay, or will he have to find the strength to let her fly?

* * * *

Wicked Force: A Wicked Horse Vegas/Big Sky Novella
By Sawyer Bennett

From *New York Times* and *USA Today* bestselling author Sawyer Bennett…

Joslyn Meyers has taken the celebrity world by storm, drawing the attention of millions. But one fan's affections has gone too far, and she's running to the one place she hopes he'll never find her – back home to Cunningham Falls.

Kynan McGrath leads The Jameson Group, a world-class security organization, and he's ready to do what it takes to keep Joslyn safe, even if it means giving up his own life in return. The one thing he's not prepared to lose, though, is his heart.

Crazy Imperfect Love: A Dirty Dicks/Big Sky Novella
By KL Grayson

From *USA Today* bestselling author KL Grayson…

Abigail Darwin needs one thing in life: consistency. Okay, make that two things: consistency and order. Tired of being shackled to her obsessive-compulsive mind, Abigail is determined to break free. Which is why she's shaking things up.

Fresh out of nursing school, she takes a traveling nurse position. A new job in a new city every few months? That's a sure-fire way to keep her from settling down and falling into old habits. First stop, Cunningham Falls, Montana.

The only problem? She didn't plan on falling in love with the quaint little town, and she sure as heck didn't plan on falling for its resident surgeon, Dr. Drake Merritt.

Laid back, messy, and spontaneous, Drake is everything she's not. But he is completely smitten by the new, quirky nurse working on the med-surg floor of the hospital.

Abby puts up a good fight, but Drake is determined to break through her carefully erected walls to find out what makes her tick. And sigh and moan and smile and laugh. Because he really loves her laugh.

But falling in love isn't part of Abby's plan. Will Drake have what it takes to convince her that the best things in life come from doing what scares us the most?

Worth Fighting For: A Warrior Fight Club/Big Sky Novella
By Laura Kaye

From *New York Times* and *USA Today* bestselling author Laura Kaye…

Getting in deep has never felt this good…

Commercial diving instructor Tara Hunter nearly lost everything in an accident that saw her medically discharged from the navy. With the help of the Warrior Fight Club, she's fought hard to overcome her fears and get back in the water where she's always felt most at home. At work, she's tough, serious, and doesn't tolerate distractions. Which is why finding her gorgeous one-night stand on her new dive team is such a problem.

Former navy deep-sea diver Jesse Anderson just can't seem to stop making mistakes—the latest being the hot-as-hell night he'd spent with his new partner. This job is his second chance, and Jesse knows he shouldn't mix business with pleasure. But spending every day with Tara's smart mouth and sexy curves makes her so damn hard to resist.

Joining a wounded warrior MMA training program seems like the perfect way to blow off steam—until Jesse finds that Tara belongs too. Now they're getting in deep and taking each other down day and night, and even though it breaks all the rules, their inescapable attraction might just be the only thing truly worth fighting for.

* * * *

Nothing Without You: A Forever Yours/Big Sky Novella
By Monica Murphy

From *New York Times* and *USA Today* bestselling author Monica Murphy...

Designing wedding cakes is Maisey Henderson's passion. She puts her heart and soul into every cake she makes, especially since she's such a believer in true love. But then Tucker McCloud rolls back into town, reminding her that love is a complete joke. The pro football player is the hottest thing to come out of Cunningham Falls—and the boy who broke Maisey's heart back in high school.

He claims he wants another chance. She says absolutely not. But Maisey's refusal is the ultimate challenge to Tucker. Life is a game, and Tucker's playing to win Maisey's heart—forever.

* * * *

All Stars Fall: A Seaside Pictures/Big Sky Novella
By Rachel Van Dyken

From *New York Times* and *USA Today* bestselling author Rachel Van Dyken...

She *left*.
Two words I can't really get out of my head.
She left *us*.
Three more words that make it that much worse.
Three being another word I can't seem to wrap my mind around.
Three kids under the age of six, and she left because she missed it. Because her dream had never been to have a family, no her dream had been to marry a rockstar and live the high life.

Moving my recording studio to Seaside Oregon seems like the best idea in the world right now especially since Seaside Oregon has turned into the place for celebrities to stay and raise families in between touring and producing. It would be lucrative to make the move, but I'm doing it for my kids because they need normal, they deserve normal. And me? Well, I just need a break and help, that too. I need a sitter and fast. Someone who won't flip me off when I ask them to sign an Iron Clad NDA, someone who won't sell our pictures to the press, and most of all? Someone who looks absolutely nothing like my ex-wife.

He's tall.
That was my first instinct when I saw the notorious Trevor Wood, drummer for the rock band Adrenaline, in the local coffee shop. He ordered a tall black coffee which made me smirk, and five minutes later I somehow agreed to interview for a nanny position. I couldn't help it; the smaller one had gum stuck in her hair while the eldest was standing on his feet and asking where babies came from. He looked so pathetic, so damn sexy and pathetic that rather than be star-struck, I took pity. I knew though; I knew the minute I signed that NDA, the minute our fingers brushed and my body became insanely aware of how close he was—I was in dangerous territory, I just didn't know how dangerous until it was too late. Until I fell for the star and realized that no matter how high they are in the sky—they're still human and fall just as hard.

* * * *

Hold On: A Play On/Big Sky Novella
By Samantha Young

From *New York Times* and *USA Today* bestselling author Samantha Young…

Autumn O'Dea has always tried to see the best in people while her big brother, Killian, has always tried to protect her from the worst. While their lonely upbringing made Killian a cynic, it isn't in Autumn's nature to be anything but warm and open. However, after a series of relationship disasters and the unsettling realization that she's drifting aimlessly through life, Autumn wonders if she's left herself too vulnerable to the world. Deciding some distance from the security blanket of her brother and an unmotivated life in Glasgow is exactly what she needs to find herself, Autumn takes up her friend's offer to stay at a ski resort in the snowy hills of Montana. Some guy-free alone time on Whitetail Mountain sounds just the thing to get to know herself better.

However, she wasn't counting on colliding into sexy Grayson King on the slopes. Autumn has never met anyone like Gray. Confident, smart, with a wicked sense of humor, he makes the men she dated seem like boys. Her attraction to him immediately puts her on the defense because being open-hearted in the past has only gotten it broken. Yet it becomes increasingly difficult to resist a man who is not only determined to seduce her, but adamant about helping her find her purpose in life and embrace the person she is. Autumn knows she shouldn't fall for Gray. It can only end badly. After all their lives are divided by an ocean and their inevitable separation is just another heart break away…

Discover 1001 Dark Nights Collection Six

DRAGON CLAIMED by Donna Grant
A Dark Kings Novella

ASHES TO INK by Carrie Ann Ryan
A Montgomery Ink: Colorado Springs Novella

ENSNARED by Elisabeth Naughton
An Eternal Guardians Novella

EVERMORE by Corinne Michaels
A Salvation Series Novella

VENGEANCE by Rebecca Zanetti
A Dark Protectors/Rebels Novella

ELI'S TRIUMPH by Joanna Wylde
A Reapers MC Novella

CIPHER by Larissa Ione
A Demonica Underworld Novella

RESCUING MACIE by Susan Stoker
A Delta Force Heroes Novella

ENCHANTED by Lexi Blake
A Masters and Mercenaries Novella

TAKE THE BRIDE by Carly Phillips
A Knight Brothers Novella

INDULGE ME by J. Kenner
A Stark Ever After Novella

THE KING by Jennifer L. Armentrout
A Wicked Novella

QUIET MAN by Kristen Ashley
A Dream Man Novella

ABANDON by Rachel Van Dyken
A Seaside Pictures Novella

THE OPEN DOOR by Laurelin Paige
A Found Duet Novella

CLOSER by Kylie Scott
A Stage Dive Novella

SOMETHING JUST LIKE THIS by Jennifer Probst
A Stay Novella

BLOOD NIGHT by Heather Graham
A Krewe of Hunters Novella

TWIST OF FATE by Jill Shalvis
A Heartbreaker Bay Novella

MORE THAN PLEASURE YOU by Shayla Black
A More Than Words Novella

WONDER WITH ME by Kristen Proby
A With Me In Seattle Novella

THE DARKEST ASSASSIN by Gena Showalter
A Lords of the Underworld Novella

Also from 1001 Dark Nights:
DAMIEN by J. Kenner
A Stark Novel

About Kristen Proby

New York Times and USA Today bestselling author Kristen Proby has published more than thirty romance novels. She is best known for her self-published With Me In Seattle and Boudreaux series, and also works with William Morrow on the Fusion Series. Kristen lives in Montana with her husband and two cats.

Discover More Kristen Proby

Tempting Brooke
A Big Sky Novella
By Kristen Proby

Brooke's Blooms has taken Cunningham Falls by surprise. The beautiful, innovative flower shop is trendy, with not only gorgeous flower arrangements, but also fun gifts for any occasion. This store is Brooke Henderson's deepest joy, and it means everything to her, which shows in how completely she and her little shop have been embraced by the small community of Cunningham Falls.

So, when her landlord dies and Brody Chabot saunters through her door, announcing that the building has been sold, and will soon be demolished, Brooke knows that she's in for the fight of her life. But she hasn't gotten this far by sitting back and quietly doing what she's told. *Hustle* is Brooke's middle name, and she has no intention of losing this fight, no matter how tempting Brody's smile -- and body -- is.

* * * *

No Reservations
A Fusion Novella
By Kristen Proby

Chase MacKenzie is *not* the man for Maura Jenkins. A self-proclaimed life-long bachelor, and unapologetic about his distaste for monogamy, a woman would have to be a masochist to want to fall into Chase's bed.

And Maura is no masochist.

Chase has one strict rule: no strings attached. Which is fine with Maura because she doesn't even really *like* Chase. He's arrogant, cocky, and let's not forget bossy. But when he aims that crooked grin at her, she goes weak in the knees. Not that she has any intentions of falling for his charms.

Definitely not.

Well, maybe just once…

* * * *

Easy For Keeps
A Boudreaux Novella
By Kristen Proby

Adam Spencer loves women. All women. Every shape and size, regardless of hair or eye color, religion or race, he simply enjoys them all. Meeting more than his fair share as the manager and head bartender of The Odyssey, a hot spot in the heart of New Orleans' French Quarter, Adam's comfortable with his lifestyle, and sees no reason to change it. A wife and kids, plus the white picket fence are not in the cards for this confirmed bachelor. Until a beautiful woman, and her sweet princess, literally knock him on his ass.

Sarah Cox has just moved to New Orleans, having accepted a position as a social worker specializing in at-risk women and children. It's a demanding, sometimes dangerous job, but Sarah is no shy wallflower. She can handle just about anything that comes at her, even the attentions of one sexy Adam Spencer. Just because he's charmed her daughter, making her think of magical kingdoms with happily ever after, doesn't mean that Sarah believes in fairy tales. But the more time she spends with the enchanting man, the more he begins to sway her into believing in forever.

Even so, when Sarah's job becomes more dangerous than any of them bargained for, will she be ripped from Adam's life forever?

* * * *

Easy With You
A With You In Seattle Novella
By Kristen Proby

Nothing has ever come easy for Lila Bailey. She's fought for every good thing in her life during every day of her thirty-one years. Aside from that one night with an impossible to deny stranger a year ago, Lila is the epitome of responsible.

Steadfast. Strong.

She's pulled herself out of the train wreck of her childhood, proud to be a professor at Tulane University and laying down roots in a city she's grown to love. But when some of her female students are viciously murdered, Lila's shaken to the core and unsure of whom she can trust in New Orleans. When the police detective assigned to the murder case comes to investigate, she's even more surprised to find herself staring into the eyes of the man that made her toes curl last year.

In an attempt to move on from the tragic loss of his wife, Asher Smith moved his daughter and himself to a new city, ready for a fresh start. A damn fine police lieutenant, but new to the New Orleans force, Asher has a lot to prove to his colleagues and himself.

With a murderer terrorizing the Tulane University campus, Asher finds himself toe-to-toe with the one woman that haunts his dreams. His hands, his lips, his body know her as intimately as he's ever known anyone. As he learns her mind and heart as well, Asher wants nothing more than to keep her safe, in his bed, and in his and his daughter's lives for the long haul.

But when Lila becomes the target, can Asher save her in time, or will he lose another woman he loves?

On behalf of 1001 Dark Nights,

Liz Berry and M.J. Rose would like to thank ~

Steve Berry
Doug Scofield
Kim Guidroz
Jillian Stein
Social Butterfly PR
Dan Slater
Asha Hossain
Chris Graham
Fedora Chen
Chelle Olson
Jessica Johns
Dylan Stockton
Richard Blake
and Simon Lipskar

Made in the USA
Middletown, DE
13 March 2019